CHOSEN BY
Jacqueline Wilson

PAWS AND WHISKERS

ANIMAL TALES FROM JACQUELINE WILSON,
MICHAEL MORPURGO, ENID BLYTON AND MORE!

ILLUSTRATED BY
NICK SHARRATT

DOUBLEDAY

PAWS AND WHISKERS
A DOUBLEDAY BOOK 978 0 857 53352 4
TRADE PAPERBACK 978 0 857 53353 1

Published in Great Britain by Doubleday,
an imprint of Random House Children's Publishers UK
A Random House Group Company

This edition published 2014

5 7 9 10 8 6 4

The Random House Group Limited supports The Forest Stewardship
Council® (FSC®), the leading international forest-certification organisation.
Our books carrying the FSC label are printed on FSC®-certified paper.
FSC is the only forest-certification scheme supported by the leading
environmental organisations, including Greenpeace. Our
paper procurement policy can be found at
www.randomhouse.co.uk/environment

MIX
Paper from
responsible sources
FSC® C016897

Set in 12/17pt New Century Schoolbook

Random House Children's Publishers UK,
61–63 Uxbridge Road, London W5 5SA

www.randomhousechildrens.co.uk
www.totallyrandombooks.co.uk
www.randomhouse.co.uk

Addresses for companies within The Random House Group Limited
can be found at: www.randomhouse.co.uk/offices.htm

THE RANDOM HOUSE GROUP Limited Reg. No. 954009

A CIP catalogue record for this book is available from the British Library.

Printed and bound in Great Britain by Clays Ltd, St Ives plc

For Natalie

CONTENTS

PETS' CORNER

DOG STORIES

PERMISSIONS

FOREWORD

Do you have a cat or a dog? When I was a little girl, I desperately wanted a pet, but we lived in a council flat and there was a strict rule that we weren't allowed to have animals. I suppose we *might* have been allowed to have a goldfish, but they're not the most responsive pets in the world. I wanted a furry little animal I could cuddle.

I made a big fuss of my best friend's cat and begged to take my godmother's dog for a walk, but it wasn't quite the same as having my *own* pet. I started collecting little china ornaments of cats and dogs, who went for walks up and down my bedroom windowsill. Then my mum gave me a toy Pekinese dog for a special summer holiday present. He was life-size and very realistic-looking. I adored him on sight and called him Vip – short for Very Important Person.

He slept in my arms at night and I carried him everywhere during the day. Not to school, of course – I didn't want to be teased. But Vip came to the shops with me and out to play with special friends. He even attended birthday parties – and got fed lots of extra sausages on sticks!

I vowed that as soon as I was grown up I'd have a real dog and a real cat – but it's actually taken me a long time to achieve my ambition. I've lived in small flats where it wouldn't be fair to keep a pet, and then I've travelled a great deal, without anyone at home to look after a little animal. But now I'm much more of a home-bird, and at long last I've got the right sort of house for pets.

I decided to start with cats, as they're more independent than dogs and don't mind too much if you have to go out to give a talk or do a book-signing. I started to research all the different breeds of cat and considered having a pedigree kitten. But then I thought about all the unwanted little cats in rescue centres – small Tracy Beaker type cats, desperate to find a loving home.

I went to the wonderful Battersea Dogs and Cats Home and wandered around their spacious cat cabins, looking for someone really special. There were cats of all sizes and colours and types, so I was totally spoiled for choice. I went from one to another, liking them all, wondering how I was ever going to choose. And then, right at the end, I saw a small grey and white kitten – and I fell instantly in love.

My boy Jacob is four now, and the sweetest, most affectionate cat ever. I've given him a little sister, Lily, also from Battersea. She came to us as a very bedraggled kitten, who'd been abandoned and had been very ill. She still has a few problems but you'd never know it – she's the most lively, funny little girl who dashes around everywhere. She totally adores Jacob and cuddles up close to him at night. He's very protective of her. When she first started going outdoors, he trotted along beside her, watching her every step – and when she suddenly darted up a tree and got stuck, he followed her and demonstrated how to climb down in a tactful and brotherly manner.

In a little while I think it will be time to get a dog at last – a small one who doesn't mind cats. I'll go to Battersea and see who I can find, and then my family will be complete.

Jacqueline Wilson

CAT STORIES

LEONIE'S PET CAT

by Jacqueline Wilson

I had great fun writing Leonie's Pet Cat. *I thought it would be a very short story, just a few pages, but it got longer and longer. It's more like a tiny novel now. I rather like Leonie. I might write some more about her one day.*

If you've read my book Clean Break, *you'll recognize one of the other characters in the story – a certain Jenna Williams. She's a children's author like me. She looks rather like me too (apart from her earrings), and now she has a kitten called Lulu who bears more than a passing resemblance to my little Lily.*

Jω

🐾 LEONIE'S PET CAT 🐾

It's so awful being the new girl at school.

'Don't worry, Leonie, I'm sure you'll make heaps of friends,' said Mum.

I *had* heaps of friends at my old school. I didn't have to try to *make* friends. They were just there – Maddy and Kas and Janie. We'd been playing together ever since we crayoned cards and finger-painted in Form One. But that was in the old days, when I lived with Dad as well as Mum. We had a proper house, with a bedroom for me (blue, with a rainbow painted on one wall) and a bedroom for my little brother Jumbo (yellow, with lions and tigers and elephants paraded on a frieze).

Now I hardly ever get to see Dad. I see all too much of Jumbo because we have to share this titchy little bedroom (*beige*, because we haven't got the time or the money to decorate just yet). Jumbo drives me crackers because he messes about with all my things. He tries to draw with my felt tips and nearly always breaks them. He pulls all my Jenna Williams stories off their special shelf and scrumples the pages. He only likes *Thomas the Tank Engine* books. He natters all the time, talking to his irritating imaginary friend Harry. He even keeps me awake at night, wheezing and snuffling because of his asthma.

Mum worried about *Jumbo* making friends. He's always been an odd little boy, very small and skinny, with big sticky-out ears and a high-pitched voice. I think the boys in the infants at our new school *do* pick on him a bit, but Jumbo doesn't care. He plays in the Wendy House with all the girls and they make a big fuss of him and invite him to their pretend tea parties. They even lay an extra cup and plate for non-existent Harry.

I can't seem to make any kind of friend, girls or boys. My new teacher, Miss Horsefield, told Keira Summers to be my friend and look after me the first day. Keira was all nicey-nicey to me in front of Miss Horsefield, and lent me her spare pen and showed me the way they do dates and margins in this class – but when I followed her out into the playground at lunch time, she hissed, 'Push off, new girl,' and ran away to play with her own friends.

That's the trouble. Everyone in our class has got friends already. They're all in little groups and gangs, and none of them seem to want me. There's one girl I really like – Julie. She's got lovely long fair hair and she wears five friendship bracelets on one wrist, and every now and then if she sees me looking she smiles at me.

'Well, smile back and make friends with her,' said Mum.

Mum doesn't understand. It's so difficult. You can't just march up to someone, grin like a lunatic, and say, 'Will you be my friend?' And even if Julie *wanted* to be my friend, she's already got all these *other* friends – horrid Keira and Rosie and Emily and Harpreet and Anya. They always play together and whisper stuff and write things down in a special book. I've tried edging up close to see exactly what they're doing, but they always go into a huddle, turning their backs on me.

But then one day Julie looked up and saw me, and she smiled again. 'Hi, Leonie,' she said.

'Hi, Julie,' I said. My mouth was so dry my voice came out in a squeak.

I hesitated, fidgeting from one foot to the other. The other girls all stared at me.

'Look, buzz off, Leonie, we're having a private meeting of our club,' said Keira.

I swallowed. 'Can't I be in your club?'

The girls all looked at each other. Keira wrinkled her nose. 'Our club's full up,' she said.

But Julie gave her a little push. 'Oh, don't be a meanie, Keira. Let's have Leonie in the club too,' she said.

'No!' said Keira.

'*Yes!*' said Julie. 'I vote Leonie gets to be a member. Hands up everyone who agrees!'

Rosie put her hand up. Then Anya and Harpreet. Emily's hand hovered, halfway up. Keira glared at her and she put it down again.

'There – Emily and I say no,' said Keira.

'But us four say yes, so we win,' said Julie. 'Welcome to the Pet Girls Club, Leonie!'

'Thank you!' I said.

'We have special badges and we swap photos of our pets and write about them in our book,' said Julie. 'I've got a Jack Russell terrier called Bobo. He's terribly naughty but I love him to bits.'

'I've just got a budgie called Joey, but he's very

clever and can go up and down his ladder for titbits,' said Rosie.

'I've got a baby rabbit called Woffles. She's got floppy ears. She's so cute,' said Harpreet.

'I've got a hamster called Twitchy,' said Anya, twitching her own nose.

'I've got two cats called Salt and Pepper,' said Emily. 'They're tortoiseshell.'

'I've got a Labrador called Dustbin because he eats all sorts of rubbish,' said Keira. She looked at me, her eyes narrowed. 'You have *got* a pet, haven't you, Leonie? Otherwise you can't be in our club, whether you want to or not.'

I hesitated a fraction too long.

'There, she hasn't got a pet!' Keira crowed. 'So you've *got* to buzz off now, Leonie Loser New Girl.'

'Shut up, Keira!' said Julie. She looked at me. 'Haven't you really got any pets, Leonie? It can be any kind of animal or bird. Maybe even a goldfish . . .'

'Goldfish don't count!' said Keira. She made stupid 'o's with her mouth, imitating a goldfish. 'They don't have any personality whatsoever and you can't cuddle them.'

'You can't really cuddle budgies, but my Joey's got heaps of personality,' said Rosie indignantly.

My heart was going *thump thump thump* underneath my new school sweatshirt. I didn't have a pet, not even a goldfish – not so much as a titchy tadpole. I wanted a pet desperately. I particularly loved cats, with their soft slinky bodies and delicate ears. But I was never able to have one. First of all my dad said he was allergic to cats. Then he left us and we had to move to the flat, and we might have been able to have a cat then, only of course Jumbo is allergic to practically *everything* and Mum said she wouldn't risk it.

'Go on, Leonie, get lost,' said Keira triumphantly.

'I've got a cat,' I blurted.

'No, you haven't!'

'Yes I have so,' I said, but I knew I sounded doubtful.

'I bet you mean you've got a *toy* cat,' said Keira.

My face felt very hot. I hoped I wasn't blushing. I had been thinking of my white furry cat nightdress-case.

Julie was looking sad. 'Toys don't really count, Leonie,' she said gently.

'She's not a toy. She's real. She's not a proper cat yet, she's a little kitten. My mum got her for me because we've had to move. She's lovely. She's got bags of personality and she's ever so cuddly. She's the best pet ever,' I lied desperately.

Julie was smiling from ear to ear. 'Why didn't you *say*? What's her name?'

I thought hard. My favourite author, Jenna Williams, had a new kitten. I'd seen a photo of it in a girls' magazine. She'd called her Lulu.

'My kitten's called Lulu,' I said.

'Oh, that's a lovely name,' said Julie. 'Right, let's write Lulu's name in our Pet Book. We'll need a full description of her – and can you bring a photo of her to school tomorrow so we can stick it in our book?'

'Yes, of course,' I said, swallowing hard.

'So you're an official member of our Pet Girls Club now. Rosie, can you make Leonie one of our badges?'

Rosie cut a circle out of cardboard, inked a big PG on the front, and attached a safety pin to the back. I pinned my badge on my sweatshirt with pride. Julie showed me their special book and I admired every-one's pets. Well, I wasn't very enthusiastic about Dustbin the Labrador because I didn't like Keira and it was plain she still couldn't stand me. But I was a proper Pet Girl now, and there was nothing she could do about it.

I was friends with Rosie and Harpreet and Anya and even Emily. I was maybe almost *best* friends with Julie, because she moved her desk nearer to mine in class and sent me little notes, and when we came out of school she skipped along beside me, her long hair flying out behind her.

'Bye, Leonie,' she said. 'Remember to bring Lulu's photo tomorrow! I'm *so* glad you're a Pet Girl now.'

'So am I,' I said.

Mum was waiting by the gate to pick me up. She was holding Jumbo's right hand. He had his left hand out, holding invisible Harry.

'My goodness, you look happy for once!' said Mum. 'Who was that pretty fair girl you were talking to?'

'That's Julie. She's my friend,' I said.

'There! I knew you'd make friends soon enough.'

'We're in a secret club,' I said proudly. Then I paused. 'Mum? Do you think I could possibly have a kitten?'

'Oh, Leonie! You know Jumbo's allergic,' she said.

'Yes, but a kitten's only little, and I'll keep it out of Jumbo's way. And I know we haven't got much money now, but I could buy all the kitten food out of my pocket money – and I could eat my cornflakes dry and the kitten could have my milk and—'

'No,' said Mum.

'But—'

'No. I'm sorry, love, but it's just not possible. Maybe in a few years' time, if Jumbo's asthma gets better.'

I didn't need a kitten in a few years' time. I needed a kitten right this instant.

'They won't let me stay in the club if I don't have a kitten,' I said.

'What? Well, then, it's a very silly club and you don't want to be in it,' said Mum.

She didn't understand at all. I desperately wanted to stay in the Pet Girls Club. I had to keep on pretending I had a kitten. If Keira found out I'd been lying, she'd be incredibly mean and crowing and have me kicked out in a nanosecond. Julie might protest, but she wouldn't be able to do anything about it.

I had to keep on lying. I couldn't take a photo of Lulu because she didn't exist. I wondered about saying we simply didn't have a camera, but they'd all wonder why I couldn't take a photo with Mum's mobile phone. I decided to be crafty.

After tea I spent a long time in my bedroom *drawing* a kitten. I don't want to sound as if I'm boasting, but I am very good at drawing. I found the photo of Jenna Williams with her kitten. I copied Lulu very carefully, and then coloured my picture with my best felt tips. I spent ages with the grey pen, inking in hundreds of little dashes to make the kitten look extra furry.

Jumbo kept pestering me, trying to see what I was drawing.

'Go *away*, Jumbo. I'm busy – can't you see?' I said irritably.

'Please let me look, Leonie,' he said. 'I love looking at your drawings. You're so good at doing pictures.'

Jumbo has this knack of saying exactly the right thing to get his own way. I let him have a look and he clapped his hands.

'It's ever so good. I love that little cat,' he said.

'She's my kitten. She's called Lulu,' I said.

'I like her. Can I stroke her?' said Jumbo, and he very gently touched the drawing with one finger.

'Watch out! Wipe your hand on your T-shirt, it's all sticky,' I said, but I let him stroke Lulu. I even made funny purring sounds. The good thing about having an odd little brother is that you can play all sorts of pretend games and nobody teases you for being babyish.

'I want a pet too!' said Jumbo. 'Draw me a pet, Leonie, go on.'

'I'm a bit sick of drawing now. My hand aches after doing all that fur,' I said.

Jumbo wouldn't give up. '*Please* will you draw me a pet, Leonie? That way it's fair – you can have one and I can have one. Go on. I'd absolutely love a pet.'

You just have to do whatever Jumbo wants.

'Do you want a kitten too?'

'No, I want a *big* pet.'

'A dog?'

'No, I want a pet I can ride!'

'A horse?'

'Bigger than a horse. I want an elephant as a pet. Go on, Leonie, draw me a great big elephant!'

So I had to draw him his elephant, and then I had to pretend to feed the elephant with buns and make trumpeting elephant noises until I was hoarse. I felt tired out when I went to bed and fell asleep almost immediately – but I woke up in the middle of the night worrying whether I would still be allowed into the Pet Girls Club without a photograph.

I kept seeing Keira saying, 'Push off, Leonie. You're a wicked liar and we aren't ever letting you into our club,' while all the other Pet Girls shook their fists at me – even Julie. I had to climb into bed with Jumbo and hug him for comfort to get back to sleep.

I took my drawing of Lulu to school with me, carefully tucked inside my project folder.

'Hi, Leonie! Have you remembered to bring your photo?' Julie asked, as soon as I went into the playground.

'I haven't got any,' I said, sighing. 'My dad's got all the photos, and he lives miles and miles away now and we hardly ever see him.'

Keira narrowed her eyes suspiciously but Julie nodded, and Rosie even put her arm round me.

'My mum and dad have split up too,' she said. 'It sucks, doesn't it?'

'Can't you take a new photo?' said Keira.

'My dad's got the camera too.'

'Take one with your mobile, silly,' said Keira.

'I haven't *got* a mobile. We haven't got much money now, see,' I said.

'Use your mum's mobile, then,' Keira went on relentlessly.

'It's such an old granny one it can't take photos. I wish you'd stop going on about it, Keira. Look, I've done a drawing of Lulu instead,' I said, brandishing it.

'Oh wow!' said Julie. 'You're brilliant at drawing, Leonie!'

'I thought *I* was ace at drawing but you're heaps better,' said Harpreet.

'It looks just like real fur!' said Anya.

'You're ever so good at drawing cats,' said Emily. 'Do you think you could do a drawing of Salt and Pepper for me?'

Keira said nothing at all. I'd settled *her* hash.

I had a wonderful day at school. I sat with Julie and the other Pet Girls at lunch, and then we all huddled up together, looking through our special Pet

Book. Julie produced a glue stick from her school bag and carefully stuck my picture of Lulu onto a fresh page.

Then I wrote out a detailed description of her, listing all her special likes and dislikes. I'd imagined her so vividly in my head that I found this easy-peasy.

'Lulu likes her toy mouse, and she likes chasing her little ball, and best of all she likes climbing up the curtains, though my mum goes mad when she does it. And she *doesn't* like loud, noisy things like vacuum cleaners, and she doesn't like water – she cried when she fell in my bath one day,' I said happily.

'Oh, she sounds adorable!' said Julie. 'Bobo doesn't climb the curtains, but he's chewed all the hems, he's so naughty. I'd love it if they could meet up, my Bobo and your Lulu – but I think he'd probably chase her. He barks like crazy when he sees our neighbour's cat.'

'Salt and Pepper would like Lulu – they're very kind to little kittens. They'd be like her auntie and uncle,' said Emily.

'I *think* my Woffles would like Lulu,' said Harpreet.

'Poor Twitchy wouldn't!' said Anya.

'Neither would Joey!' said Rosie. 'When my gran

comes to stay with her cat Tabitha, we can't ever let him out of his bird cage, just in case.'

'Dustbin would quite definitely chase her – and catch her too,' said Keira with unnecessary relish.

'No, he wouldn't catch her. Lulu can run like the wind. She'd run to me and clamber up into my arms and I'd keep her safe,' I said, feeling ultra protective of Lulu – almost forgetting she wasn't real.

Each day I told the Pet Girls a new made-up anecdote about Lulu. I told them how she hid in the airing cupboard, how she climbed up the bookcase, how she knocked over all the photos on the mantelpiece, how she curled up beside me on my pillow at night – and they all hung on my every word.

'Could I perhaps come to your house and play after school and meet Lulu?' Julie asked, putting her arm round me.

I didn't know what to say. I desperately wanted Julie to come and play, but I couldn't produce a kitten out of thin air.

'I'd love that, Julie, but I'm afraid Mum says I can't have anyone round at the moment,' I said anxiously.

'Oh, that's a pity,' said Julie.

'*Why* won't your mum let you have friends round to play?' asked Keira.

'Oh, Keira! I expect Leonie's mum is feeling a bit

stressed,' said Rosie. 'I know my mum was miserable for ages. You have to make allowances.'

They were such kind girls – all except Keira. She had a way of staring at me as if she could look straight into my head and see all the lies and worries tangled up inside, like skeins of knitting wool. She was the only one who still seemed very suspicious.

I tried hard to think of some way I could convince her. That evening I rifled through the magazine again and found the photo of Jenna Williams and Lulu. I got my scissors and carefully snipped around Lulu. There, I had one little photo of my kitten! But it was clear I'd cut it out of a magazine because there were a lot of words on the back. I thought hard and then fished around in my jewellery box. I had a little silver locket Dad had bought me as a birthday present. I hadn't worn it for ages because I didn't like my dad any more. But now I prised it open and dug out the photo inside – one of Dad holding me when I was a baby. I snipped away at the photo of Lulu until it fitted exactly, and then slotted it in place inside the locket. It looked perfect.

I wore my locket to school the next day, tucking it away underneath my school sweatshirt. I waited until playtime, and then when all the Pet Girls gathered together I fished my locket out.

'I *have* got a photo of Lulu after all,' I said. 'I just remembered last night. There's this one in my special locket.'

I opened it up and showed them. Everyone made special 'Aaaah' noises – except Keira.

'See, Keira!' I said, thrusting the locket under her nose.

'Mmm,' she said.

She *still* didn't look utterly convinced. I didn't like the way she was looking at me. There was a weird gleam in her eye, but she didn't say anything else.

My heart turned over the next morning at school. Keira was waving an old magazine around.

'Look what's in here,' she said, opening up the magazine and stabbing at the page with her finger.

All the Pet Girls peered at it curiously.

'That's Jenna Williams. I've got some of her books,' said Julie.

'She's got a lovely little kitten,' said Rosie.

'Yes. And guess what her kitten is called!' said Keira.

'It says she's called Lulu – just like your kitten, Leonie!' said Harpreet.

'What a coincidence,' said Anya.

'Coincidence, my bottom!' said Keira. 'It's not a coincidence at all. Show us that picture in your locket,

Leonie, go on. Then we can all see for ourselves. That *isn't* your kitten! It's Jenna Willams' own cat. I *knew* you were fibbing – and then I found the photo last night in my sister's mag. You're just a pathetic little liar, Leonie. You can't be in our Pet Girls Club because you haven't got a pet – so push off!'

Julie and the others were staring at me, stunned.

'I'm sure you've made a mistake, Keira,' said Julie anxiously. 'Let's see your photo again, Leonie.'

'Yes, go on, we'll prove it,' said Keira, tugging at the chain of my locket.

'Stop it! You'll break it if you're not careful,' I said, struggling.

It was no use. Keira's hard little fingers scrabbled at my neck, then she opened the locket with her thumbnail and poked my photo out. She held it up triumphantly for all to see the printing on the back.

'There! See!' she said, her face pink with triumph.

They all saw.

'Oh, Leonie,' said Julie sorrowfully.

'You fibber!' said Emily, looking outraged.

'I'm not, I'm not,' I said. I couldn't bear it. It had been so wonderful to be Julie's friend and one of the Pet Girls gang. I thought desperately hard.

'All right, I did tell a little bit of a fib,' I said. 'Lulu isn't exactly *my* kitten. You're right, Keira, she does belong to Jenna Williams. But she lets me play with her lots and says she can be partly mine too.'

'What rubbish!' said Keira. 'As if Jenna Williams would say that!'

'Do you really know Jenna Williams, Leonie?' asked Julie.

'Yes! I know her ever so well because . . . because Jenna Williams is my granny!' I said.

They all stared at me, mouths open.

'She never is!' said Keira.

'She is, she is!'

'Well, why didn't you say so before?' said Emily.

'Because I'm not allowed. Jenna Williams – Granny – likes to be completely private. But I go to stay with her lots and I play with Lulu there,' I insisted.

'You must think we're total nutcases to believe such rubbish!' said Keira.

'As if you'd ever have a rich and famous granny like Jenna Williams!' said Emily.

'We don't believe a word of it,' said Harpreet.

'Your tongue must be really black, telling all those lies,' said Anya.

Julie didn't say anything at all – but she looked desperately disappointed.

'It's true, really it is!' I said, my eyes starting to prickle with tears.

'Oh look, she's going to cry now! What a baby!' said Keira. 'Come on, everyone. We don't want to play with stupid liars.'

They went off and left me, even Julie. I couldn't stop the tears spilling down my cheeks then.

Mum saw I'd been crying when she came to collect me from school.

'What's up, lovey?' she said.

I felt my eyes stinging again. 'Nothing,' I mumbled.

Julie hurried past, barely looking at me.

'Oh dear,' said Mum. 'Have you fallen out with Julie?'

'Yes,' I whispered. 'Come on. Let's go *home*.' I felt as if everyone was staring at me, probably pointing.

'Well, I'm sure you'll make it up with her. Or maybe you can pal up with some of the other girls,' Mum said brightly.

'No I can't,' I said thickly, in floods of tears now. 'They all hate and despise me and I haven't got any friends at all.'

'I've got heaps of friends,' said Jumbo, which made me cry even harder.

'Why on earth would they hate and despise you, Leonie?' said Mum.

'Because they think I'm a liar – and I *am*,' I howled.

'Whatever have you said?' Mum asked, giving me a tissue.

'I said I had a kitten, so I could be in their Pet Girls Club and I haven't,' I wailed.

'Oh goodness, that's not a really terrible lie,' said Mum. 'Can't you explain you really *want* a kitten and you just got carried away?'

'But I told lots of stories about her. And I said . . . I said Jenna Williams was my granny!'

'What?' Mum struggled to keep her face straight.

'You're laughing at me!' I said, outraged.

'Well, you must admit, it is funny. Oh darling, you're such a ninny. Stop crying now. I'm sure you'll make some new friends soon,' said Mum.

'You can have some of *my* friends if you like,' said Jumbo.

'I don't want any of your silly little friends. I don't want to make any new friends. I just want to be best friends with Julie and be in the Pet Girls Club,' I wept.

Mum made smoothies and jam sandwiches when we got home, but I said I didn't want any and flounced off to the bedroom. Jumbo tried to follow me but I shut him out.

I had a good cry all by myself, and then, when I was at the sniffly, hiccupping stage, I switched on my computer and went on the Jenna Williams fan club website to try to cheer myself up a bit. There was a little image of Lulu the kitten, and if you clicked on it she skittered all around the screen, making the cutest little *mew-mew-mew* noises.

I looked up the reviews of the latest Jenna Williams book and then I clicked on her daily blog. She was being very comforting to a girl who had emailed her to say she had no friends.

'Well, *I* haven't got any friends either,' I muttered.

I sat nibbling my lip, wondering whether to try emailing Jenna Williams myself. I had sent her a couple of messages before, telling her how much I liked her books, but she'd never replied. The website explained that she couldn't reply to everyone, though she did read every single message.

'Read *my* message then, Jenna Williams,' I said, and started typing.

Dear Jenna Williams,

I feel such a fool writing to you, but I hope you might understand. I was so desperate to be in this Pet Girls Club at my new school that I pretended I had a kitten. I can't have any pets because my little brother has allergies. I pretended I had a kitten just like your Lulu. Then I took a picture of Lulu to school, but this really nasty girl Keira recognized it. They all turned on me then and said I couldn't be in their club, and so I did a mad thing and said you were my granny and that you let me share Lulu. They didn't believe me, and now I don't know what to do. They all know I'm a liar and I feel awful. If I was a girl in one of your books you'd find a way to make it all come right. That's why books are better than real life.

Love from Leonie

I blushed beetroot red as I typed, unable to believe I'd been such an idiot – but I felt just a little bit better when I'd finished. I wasn't absolutely sure Jenna Williams herself would ever read my message, but at least I'd confessed.

I went and had my smoothie and sandwich after all, and then I played with Jumbo because I felt bad that I'd shut him out. I drew him a comic strip about his pet elephant, and then he coloured it in with his wax crayons. He went over the lines and spoiled it rather, but I didn't point this out.

Mum made us spaghetti for supper, and Jumbo and I played the slurp-slurp game and Mum didn't get cross. I still felt pretty miserable though. I felt sick at the thought of facing all the Pet Girls tomorrow morning.

At bedtime I went to switch off my computer and

saw that I had a message. It wasn't from one of my friends at my old school. It wasn't from my dad. It wasn't from my real granny in Scotland. *It was a message from Jenna Williams!*

Dear Leonie,

Oh dear, you've got yourself in a bit of a pickle, haven't you! I do understand though. I sometimes pretended things at school and then got into trouble too. It's a blessing to have a vivid imagination – but it can also be a curse!

Whereabouts do you live? I've got a new book coming out shortly called *My Kitten Lulu*, and I'm touring all over the country promoting it. Maybe you could come and see me and meet Lulu?

Love from 'Granny' Williams x

I gave such a scream that Mum came charging into the bedroom, terrified.

'What on earth's the matter now, Leonie? You scared me half to death!'

'Look! I can't believe it! Jenna Williams has replied to me!' I shouted. 'Oh, Mum, she wants me to meet Lulu! Please, please, please, can we go to see her?'

'What? I don't think it can be the *real* Jenna Williams. And we can't go hiking all over the country to go and see her,' said Mum.

'Look, she's doing a big event in London!' I said, stabbing at the screen. 'We could go there. Oh please, Mum.'

'Please, please, Mum,' said Jumbo sleepily from under his Dumbo duvet, though he didn't really have a clue what I was talking about.

'Well,' said Mum, wavering, 'I suppose we *could* have a day out in London for a treat. All right. We'll go and see your Jenna Williams and her blessed kitten if it means so much to you, Leonie.'

'It means the whole world,' I said solemnly.

I wrote and told Jenna Williams exactly that.

Dear Jenna Williams,

Is it really YOU? I can't believe you've actually replied. You've made me feel soooo much better! Please may I really come and see you when you're in London? And will Lulu really be there too? Will I be able to stroke her?

I don't mind so much not having any friends now. I feel that you are my friend. I'm so glad you're not cross with me for pretending you're my granny. I still wish you were.

Love from Leonie

There was another email waiting for me in the morning.

Dear Leonie,

I'm so glad you've cheered up. I'm doing the London talk at two o'clock. If you and your mum would like to come half an hour early and talk to my publicist, then you can come and see me – and Lulu too. We're both looking forward to meeting you.

Love from Jenna Williams (Granny)

I was bubbling over with happiness – but all my fizz went flat when I had to go into school. I saw Keira first. She mouthed *Liar!* at me and stalked off. Emily and Rosie and Harpreet and Anya looked a little anxious, but when Keira glared at them, they all mouthed *Liar!* too.

Julie was late getting to school. She only came through the school gate as the bell started ringing. She ran across the playground. I hung my head. I couldn't bear to see her mouth *Liar!* too.

But she didn't! She took hold of my hand and squeezed it urgently.

'Leonie! I've been thinking. I felt so bad last night. We were all so horrid to you. I think it was because you were so clever at fooling us. But we acted like you'd done something terrible and you haven't *really*. Will you still be friends?'

'Oh, Julie! Yes, I really badly want to be your friend. But I can't be a Pet Girl now, can I?'

'Probably not. But never mind. We could maybe start up our own club, just you and me.'

'Oh yes! Perhaps it could be a book club? Do you like Jenna Williams's books? Oh, Julie, wait till I tell you the most amazing thing about Jenna Williams!' I said.

'She's your granny. Not!' said Julie.

'Yeah, I know, I made that up, I was stupid – but listen, I emailed her and she wrote back to me! She wants me to come and see her and meet her kitten Lulu!' I said excitedly.

Julie didn't look at all impressed. She rolled her eyes and sighed. 'Now listen, Leonie, you're going to have to stop all this pretending stuff. You don't need to any more. We're friends and we'll have our own club. It can be a book club if you like. Just don't start making up stories because everyone will think you're barmy,' said Julie.

She didn't believe me! And if my special new friend Julie didn't believe me, then I didn't have a hope of impressing Keira and all the others. I could always print out the emails – but they could always say I'd written them myself. I decided I'd simply have to shut up about Jenna Williams at school. It seemed infuriating when at last I truly had something to boast about, but it couldn't be helped.

I rather hoped Julie would break off with Keira and the others, but she stayed friends with them too, and still spent some playtimes huddled in the corner with them writing in the Pet Book. Keira tore out the page with my drawing of Lulu, crumpled it up and tossed it in the bin. Julie waited until the bell went and then dashed over and retrieved it. She tried to smooth out the creases as best she could.

'There now. It's still a lovely drawing,' she said, giving it to me.

'If you bring me a photo of your dog, Bobo, I'll draw you a picture of him,' I offered.

'That would be great. Or tell you what, why don't you come round to my house for tea and then you can see him for yourself,' said Julie. 'Your mum won't mind if you go out to tea, will she?'

Mum was completely thrilled when I asked her after school.

'I'm so pleased you and Leonie are friends, Julie,' she said. 'Of course she can go to tea with you. And you must come to tea with us soon.'

'Oh, that will be great. I'm glad you're feeling better now,' said Julie politely.

Mum looked puzzled. I blushed. Luckily Julie

didn't say anything further. I resolved once and for all never ever to tell any fibs again.

I had a *wonderful* time at Julie's. I especially loved her funny little dog Bobo. He was incredibly naughty, and raced round and round madly, barking his head off – but then he leaped up and licked my face lovingly as if I were an ice lolly! It was quite hard to sketch him because he hardly ever kept still, but I managed to do a quick crayon drawing of him chewing Julie's dad's slipper, and the whole family acted as if it were a masterpiece.

I asked Julie back to our place two days later. I was a bit anxious because our new flat's pretty cramped and we're having to make do with grotty old carpets and curtains for the moment, and I haven't even got my own bedroom. Julie's bedroom is brilliant, a beautiful deep purple, with silver cushions in the shape of stars, and shelves all round two walls (but she hasn't got as many Jenna Williams books as I have!). Julie wasn't a bit sniffy about anything though, and she liked my mum and, weirdly, she *adored* Jumbo. I was scared he was being a bit of a pain, hanging around us and nattering away nineteen to the dozen, but Julie seemed to find him really funny.

'You're so lucky having a little brother,' she said.

'You're so lucky having a little dog,' I said. 'I'll do

a swap if you like. I'll have Bobo and you can have Jumbo.'

The only awkward moment was when we were sitting near my computer.

'Shall I just show you my Jenna Williams emails?' I said hopefully.

Julie sighed. 'Oh, Leonie!' she said, frowning.

I decided it might be better not to pursue things. Julie was clearly never going to believe me – and it was really all my own fault.

But wonderfully, it really was true. I had yet another email from Jenna Williams on Friday, the day before her big event in London.

Dear Leonie,

I'm looking forward to seeing you tomorrow. I've reserved special seats for you at the theatre. Have you made a friend at your new school yet? If so, do feel free to bring her along to keep you company.

Love from Granny

I *loved* it that she was still calling herself my granny! And now I could bring a friend! I rang Julie straight away. I didn't say Jenna Williams had specially invited me. I was sure she still wouldn't believe me.

'We've got special tickets to go to a Jenna Williams talk tomorrow, Julie. Can you come with us? Oh, I do hope you'll say yes!' I said.

Julie wasn't very sure at first, because she usually went to dancing class on Saturday – but she did get excited at the idea of hearing Jenna Williams talk.

'You really truly have tickets, Leonie?' she asked cautiously.

'Really truly, I promise,' I said.

'Then OK, yes please!' said Julie.

So we went to pick her up on Saturday morning, Mum and Jumbo and me, and then we all got the train to London. Jumbo was wild with excitement because he loves trains, and he kept tapping on the carriage window and shrieking, 'Look, there's a *train*!' whenever he saw one. He saw one all too frequently, and even Julie was a bit sick of him by the time we got to Waterloo. Then we went to a big building on the South Bank – and when we got inside, we saw a great long queue, all the way up the stairs, of girls waiting to see Jenna Williams.

'Oh goodness, look at all those girls!' said Julie. 'Come on, we'd better find the end of the queue.'

'We don't have to wait, do we, Mum?' I said.

'Apparently not,' said Mum, and she had a word

with one of the ushers in charge of the queue.

'Oh, yes, so you're Leonie!' said the usher. 'Jenna told me to look out for you. Come this way. She's in the Green Room signing some books.'

Julie was watching with her mouth open. 'You actually *do* know Jenna Williams!' she gasped. 'Oh my goodness, is she *really* your granny?'

'No, not really – but she signed herself Granny on her email, honestly,' I said. 'Oh heavens, my tummy's gone all funny! I'm really going to meet her!'

'I feel a bit wobbly too!' said Julie. 'I'm scared!'

'Harry and I think you two are daft,' said Jumbo. 'Jenna Williams is just a boring lady who writes books with lots of words. There are no pictures of trains in any of them.'

Julie and I raised our eyebrows at each other. Then we were ushered into a side room, and we felt so weird we actually held hands, clinging to each other. There was Jenna Williams sitting in a corner, signing a huge pile of books. It really was the actual Jenna Williams with her short hair and her earrings and her black clothes and her fancy boots. She smiled when she saw us.

'Hello, girls!' she said, looking at both of us. 'Leonie?'

'Yes,' I said, in a little mouse squeak.

Jenna winked at me. 'Well, come and say hi to your granny then!' she said.

Julie gasped. I giggled.

'It's OK, Jenna. I told Julie I was just fibbing and she understands,' I said.

'I'm so sorry our Leonie was so daft, Miss Williams,' said Mum. 'She gets a bit carried away sometimes.'

'It shows she's got a vivid imagination,' said Jenna. 'Perhaps you'll be a writer like me when you grow up, Leonie.' She smiled at Julie. 'What do *you* want to do for a career?'

'I love animals so I think I'd like to be a vet,' said Julie. 'But you have to be a right old brainy box, so maybe I'll work in a dog rescue shelter.'

'Ah yes, you run the famous Pet Girls Club,' said Jenna. 'Do you think Leonie could be a proper member if I grant her part ownership of my Lulu?'

'Where *is* Lulu?' I asked excitedly.

'Ah, she's having a little nap at the moment,' said Jenna. 'Come and have a peep.'

She led us to a corner of the room where there was a big plush navy basket. There, curled up on a soft furry cushion, was a small grey kitten, her head resting on her paws.

'Oh, she's beautiful!' I whispered.

'She's so cute!' said Julie.

'Can we play with her?' asked Jumbo.

'In a minute, when she's woken up properly and got used to you. Perhaps you'd like to stroke her very gently, Leonie?'

I knelt down carefully beside Lulu's basket and touched her tentatively with just the tips of my fingers. Her eyes opened and she peered up at me, showing me her little white face. I stroked her neck and she gave a wriggle – and then when I stroked her properly she started making little noises in her throat. I bent closer.

'She's purring! She likes me!' I whispered.

'Of course she likes you,' said Jenna. 'You own a little bit of her. Which bit would you like? Her tail? Her funny whiskers? I know – how about one of her little white paws?'

'That would be absolutely perfect!' I breathed.

After a few minutes Lulu jumped right out of her basket, and then we could all join in, throwing a toy mouse for her and playing a game with feathers on a stick. We fed her too, and she golloped up her saucer of chopped-up chicken and lapped at her water bowl. She tried putting her tiny paw in the water and splashed me, which made us all laugh.

Julie took heaps of photos on her mobile phone,

including a lovely one with Lulu on my lap, and Jenna sitting beside us, her arm round me. She signed a copy of her new book for me, and one for Julie too – and promised Jumbo that she'd try hard to put a train in her next book specially for him.

Then it was time for Jenna to go on stage to do her talk. She gave us all a hug and told me to email her again to let her know how I was getting on. We went to listen to her talk, sitting in special reserved seats right at the front – and then at the end an assistant carried little Lulu on stage to wave her paw at everyone.

'That's *my* paw!' I said.

It was the most wonderful day of my life. The next Monday at school was pretty special too. Julie took her mobile phone and showed Keira and Emily and Rosie and Harpreet and Anya all the photos she'd taken.

'Look, here's one of Leonie with Jenna Williams and Lulu,' said Julie proudly.

'Then . . . is Jenna Williams *really* her granny?' asked Keira.

Julie hesitated. She's not really the sort of girl who tells fibs. 'I'm not allowed to say,' she said, smiling mysteriously.

She put her arm round me and we marched off together. I don't know whether they'll let me back in the Pet Girls Club. I don't care. I have Julie as a best friend and Jenna Williams as a pretend granny, and I own a little white paw of the sweetest kitten in the world.

CATWINGS

by Ursula K. Le Guin

If you have a pet cat, you'll know they have an extraordinary ability to disappear. One minute they're right in front of you, stretching or yawning or idly washing themselves – then you read a few sentences of your book and glance up again and they've completely vanished. You look in all their favourite places around the house: the back of the sofa, the cosiest chair, the pile of ironing, under or on top of your bed, but they're not anywhere.

You wonder if they've sneaked out through the cat flap into the garden, so you go and look in every bush and peer up every tree, and they're not there either. So you repeat the whole process several times, and there's not the faintest trace of your cat. You sit down again, heart beating fast, trying not to worry but worrying anyway, in case your cat has managed to trap itself in

the basement or a neighbour's garage or has somehow strayed onto the road. And then, suddenly, there is your cat, right in front of you, miaowing nonchalantly, appearing again out of nowhere.

I've often thought cats might have the ability to make themselves invisible – but until I read Catwings by Ursula K. Le Guin I'd never thought that they might be able to fly. I absolutely love this story about four American kittens, born into a bad neighbourhood, who grow little furry wings and soar up into the air to get away from growling dogs – although the owl is a more frightening enemy.

I've checked my kitten Lily's back very carefully just in case she might be sprouting tiny furry wings. There's no sign of them so far – but you never know!

Jw

🐾 CATWINGS 🐾

1

Mrs Jane Tabby could not explain why all four of her children had wings.

'I suppose their father was a fly-by-night,' a neighbor said, and laughed unpleasantly, sneaking round the dumpster.

'Maybe they have wings because I dreamed, before they were born, that I could fly away from this neighborhood,' said Mrs Jane Tabby. 'Thelma, your face is dirty; wash it. Roger, stop hitting James. Harriet, when you purr, you should close your eyes part way and knead me with your front paws; yes, that's the way. How is the milk this morning, children?'

'It's very good, Mother, thank you,' they answered happily. They were beautiful children, well brought up. But Mrs Tabby worried about them secretly. It really was a terrible neighborhood, and getting worse. Car wheels and truck wheels rolling past all day – rubbish and litter – hungry dogs – endless shoes and boots walking, running, stamping, kicking – nowhere safe and quiet, and less and less to eat. Most of the sparrows had moved away. The rats were fierce and dangerous; the mice were shy and scrawny.

So the children's wings were the least of Mrs Tabby's worries. She washed those silky wings every day, along with chins and paws and tails, and wondered about them now and then, but she worked too hard finding food and bringing up the family to think much about things she didn't understand.

But when the huge dog chased little Harriet and cornered her behind the garbage can, lunging at her with open, white-toothed jaws, and Harriet with one desperate mew flew straight up into the air and over the dog's staring head and lighted on the rooftop – then Mrs Tabby understood.

The dog went off growling, its tail between its legs.

'Come down now, Harriet,' her mother called. 'Children, come here please, all of you.'

They all came back to the dumpster. Harriet was still trembling. The others all purred with her till she was calm, and then Mrs Jane Tabby said: 'Children, I dreamed a dream before you were born, and I see now what it meant. This is not a good place to grow up in, and you have wings to fly from it. I want you to do that. I know you've been practicing. I saw James flying across the alley last night – and yes, I saw you doing nose dives, too, Roger. I think you are ready. I want you to have a good dinner and fly away – far away.'

'But Mother—' said Thelma, and burst into tears.

'I have no wish to leave,' said Mrs Tabby quietly. 'My work is here. Mr Tom Jones proposed to me last night, and I intend to accept him. I don't want you children underfoot!'

All the children wept, but they knew that that is the way it must be, in cat families. They were proud, too, that their mother trusted them to look after themselves. So all together they had a good dinner from the garbage can that the dog had knocked over. Then Thelma, Roger, James, and Harriet purred goodbye to their dear mother, and one after another they spread their wings and flew up, over the alley, over the roofs, away.

Mrs Jane Tabby watched them. Her heart was full of fear and pride.

'They are remarkable children, Jane,' said Mr Tom Jones in his soft, deep voice.

'Ours will be remarkable too, Tom,' said Mrs Tabby.

2

As Thelma, Roger, James, and Harriet flew on, all they could see beneath them, mile after mile, was the city's roofs, the city's streets.

A pigeon came swooping up to join them. It flew along with them, peering at them uneasily from its little, round, red eye. 'What kind of birds are you, anyways?' it finally asked.

'Passenger pigeons,' James said promptly.

Harriet mewed with laughter.

The pigeon jumped in mid-air, stared at her, and then turned and swooped away from them in a great, quick curve.

'I wish I could fly like that,' said Roger.

'Pigeons are really dumb,' James muttered.

'But my wings ache already,' Roger said, and Thelma said, 'So do mine. Let's land somewhere and rest.'

Little Harriet was already heading down towards a church steeple.

They clung to the carvings of the church roof, and got a drink of water from the roof gutters.

'Sitting in the catbird seat!' sang Harriet, perched on a pinnacle.

'It looks different over there,' said Thelma, pointing her nose to the west. 'It looks softer.'

They all gazed earnestly westward, but cats don't see the distance clearly.

'Well, if it's different, let's try it,' said James, and they set off again. They could not fly with untiring ease, like the pigeons. Mrs Tabby had always seen to it that they ate well, and so they were quite plump, and had to beat their wings hard to keep their weight aloft. They learned how to glide, not beating their wings, letting the wind bear them up; but Harriet found gliding difficult, and wobbled badly.

After another hour or so they landed on the roof of a huge factory, even though the air there smelled terrible, and there they slept for a while in a weary, furry heap. Then, towards nightfall, very hungry – for nothing gives an appetite like flying – they woke and flew on.

The sun set. The city lights came on, long strings and chains of lights below them, stretching out towards darkness. Towards darkness they flew, and at last, when around them and under them everything was dark except for one light twinkling over the hill, they descended slowly from the air and landed on the ground.

A soft ground – a strange ground! The only ground they knew was pavement, asphalt, cement. This was all new to them, dirt, earth, dead leaves, grass, twigs, mushrooms, worms. It all smelled extremely interesting. A little creek ran nearby. They heard the song of it and went to drink, for they were very thirsty. After drinking, Roger stayed crouching on the bank, his nose almost in the water, his eyes gazing.

'What's that in the water?' he whispered.

The others came and gazed. They could just make out something moving in the water, in the starlight – a silvery flicker, a gleam. Roger's paw shot out . . .

'I think it's dinner,' he said.

After dinner, they curled up together again under a bush and fell asleep. But first Thelma, then Roger, then James, and then small Harriet, would lift their head, open an eye, listen a moment, on guard. They knew they had come to a much better place than the alley, but they also knew that every place is dangerous, whether you are a fish, or a cat, or even a cat with wings.

3

'It's absolutely unfair,' the thrush cried.

'Unjust!' the finch agreed.

'Intolerable!' yelled the bluejay.

'I don't see why,' a mouse said. 'You've always had wings. Now they do. What's unfair about that?'

The fish in the creek said nothing. Fish never do. Few people know what fish think about injustice, or anything else.

'I was bringing a twig to the nest just this morning, and a *cat* flew down, a cat *flew* down, from the top of the Home Oak, and *grinned* at me in mid-air!' the thrush said, and all the other songbirds cried, 'Shocking! Unheard of! Not allowed!'

'You could try tunnels,' said the mouse, and trotted off.

The birds had to learn to get along with the Flying Tabbies. Most of the birds, in fact, were more frightened and outraged than really endangered, since they were far better flyers than Roger, Thelma, Harriet, and James. The birds never got their wings tangled up in pine branches and never absent-mindedly bumped into tree trunks, and when pursued they could escape by speeding up or taking evasive action. But they were alarmed, and with good cause, about their fledglings. Many birds had eggs in the nest now; when the babies hatched, how could they be kept safe from a cat who could fly up and perch on the slenderest branch, among the thickest leaves?

It took a while for the Owl to understand this. Owl is not a quick thinker. She is a long thinker. It was late in spring, one evening, when she was gazing fondly at her two new owlets, that she saw James flitting by, chasing bats. And she slowly thought, 'This will not do . . .'

And softly Owl spread her great, gray wings, and silently flew after James, her talons opening.

The Flying Tabbies had made their nest in a hole halfway up a big elm, above fox and coyote level and too small for raccoons to get into. Thelma and Harriet were washing each other's necks and talking over the day's adventures when they heard a pitiful crying at the foot of the tree.

'James!' cried Harriet.

He was crouching under the bushes, all scratched and bleeding, and one of his wings dragged upon the ground.

'It was the Owl,' he said, when his sisters had helped him climb painfully up the tree trunk into their home hole. 'I just escaped. She caught me, but I scratched her, and she let go for a moment.'

And just then Roger came scrambling into the nest with his eyes round and black and full of fear. 'She's after me!' he cried. 'The Owl!'

They all washed James's wounds till he fell asleep.

'Now we know how the little birds feel,' said Thelma, grimly.

'What will James do?' Harriet whispered. 'Will he ever fly again?'

'He'd better not,' said a soft, large voice just outside their door. The Owl was sitting there.

The Tabbies looked at one another. They did not say a word till morning came.

At sunrise Thelma peered cautiously out. The Owl was gone. 'Until this evening,' said Thelma.

From then on they had to hunt in the daytime and hide in their nest all night; for the Owl thinks slowly, but the Owl thinks long.

James was ill for days and could not hunt at all. When he recovered, he was very thin and could not fly much, for his left wing soon grew stiff and lame. He never complained. He sat for hours in the creek, his wings folded, fishing. The fish did not complain either. They never do.

One night of early summer the Tabbies were all curled in their home hole, rather tired and discouraged. A raccoon family was quarreling loudly in the next tree. Thelma had found nothing to eat all day but a shrew, which gave her indigestion. A coyote had chased Roger away from the wood rat he had been about to catch that afternoon. James's fishing had been unsuccessful. The Owl kept flying past on silent wings, saying nothing.

Two young male raccoons in the next tree started a fight, cursing and shouting insults. The other raccoons all joined in, screeching and scratching and swearing.

'It sounds just like the old alley,' James remarked.

'Do you remember the Shoes?' Harriet asked dreamily. She was looking quite plump, perhaps because she was so small. Her sister and brothers had become thin and rather scruffy.

'Yes,' James said. 'Some of them chased me once.'

'Do you remember the Hands?' Roger asked.

'Yes,' Thelma said. 'Some of them picked me up once. When I was just a kitten.'

'What did they do – the Hands?' Harriet asked.

'They squeezed me. It hurt. And the hands person was shouting – "Wings! Wings! It has wings!" – that's what it kept shouting in its silly voice. And squeezing me.'

'What did you do?'

'I bit it,' Thelma said, with modest pride. 'I bit it, and it dropped me, and I ran back to Mother, under the dumpster. I didn't know how to fly yet.'

'I saw one today,' said Harriet.

'What? A Hands? A Shoes?' said Thelma.

'A human bean?' said James.

'A human being?' Roger said.

'Yes,' said Harriet. 'It saw me, too.'

'Did it chase you?'

'Did it kick you?'

'Did it throw things at you?'

'No. It just stood and watched me flying. And its eyes got round, just like ours.'

'Mother always said,' Thelma remarked, thoughtfully, 'that if you found the right kind of Hands, you'd never have to hunt again. But if you found the wrong kind, it would be worse than dogs, she said.'

'I think this one is the right kind,' said Harriet.

'What makes you think so?' Roger asked, sounding like their mother.

'Because it ran off and came back with a plate full of dinner,' Harriet said. 'And it put the dinner down on that big stump at the edge of the field, the field where we scared the cows that day, you know. And then it went off quite a way, and sat down, and just watched me. So I flew over and ate the dinner. It was an interesting dinner. Like what we used to get in the alley, but fresher. And,' said Harriet, sounding like their mother, 'I'm going back there tomorrow to see what's on that stump.'

'You just be careful, Harriet Tabby!' said Thelma, sounding even more like their mother.

4

The next day, when Harriet went to the big stump at the edge of the cow pasture, flying low and cautiously, she found a tin pie-plate of meat scraps and kibbled catfood waiting for her. The girl from Overhill Farm was also waiting for her, sitting about twenty feet away from the stump, and holding very still. Susan Brown was her name, and she was eight years old. She watched Harriet fly out of the woods and hover like a fat hummingbird over the stump, then settle down, fold her wings neatly, and eat. Susan Brown held her breath. Her eyes grew round.

The next day, when Harriet and Roger flew cautiously out of the woods and hovered over the stump, Susan was sitting about fifteen feet away, and beside her sat her twelve-year-old brother Hank. He had not believed a word she said about flying cats. Now his eyes were perfectly round, and he was holding his breath.

Harriet and Roger settled down to eat.

'You didn't say there were two of them,' Hank whispered to his sister.

Harriet and Roger sat on the stump licking their whiskers clean.

'You didn't say there were two of them,' Roger whispered to his sister.

'I didn't know!' both the sisters whispered back. 'There was only one, yesterday. But they look nice – don't they?'

The next day, Hank and Susan put out two pie-tins of cat dinner on the stump, then went ten steps away, sat down on the grass, and waited.

Harriet flew boldly from the woods and alighted on the stump. Roger followed her. Then – 'Oh, look!' Susan whispered – came Thelma, flying very slowly, with a disapproving expression on her face. And finally – 'Oh, look, *look*!' Susan whispered – James, flying low and lame, flapped over to the stump, landed on it, and began to eat. He ate, and ate, and ate. He even growled once at Thelma, who moved to the other pie-tin.

The two children watched the four winged cats.

Harriet, quite full, washed her face, and watched the children.

Thelma finished a last tasty kibble, washed her left front paw, and gazed at the children. Suddenly she flew up from the stump and straight at them. They ducked as she went over. She flew right round both their heads and then back to the stump.

'Testing,' she said to Harriet, James, and Roger.

'If she does it again, don't catch her,' Hank said to Susan. 'It'd scare her off.'

'You think I'm *stupid*?' Susan hissed.

They sat still. The cats sat still. Cows ate grass nearby. The sun shone.

'Kitty,' Susan said in a soft, high voice. 'Kitty kit-kit-kit-kit-kit-cat, kitty-cat, kitty-wings, kittywings, catwings!'

Harriet jumped off the stump into the air, performed a cartwheel, and flew loop-the-loop over to Susan. She landed on Susan's shoulder and sat there, holding on tight and purring in Susan's ear.

'I will never never never ever catch you, or cage you, or do anything to you you don't want me to do,' Susan said to Harriet. 'I promise. Hank, you promise too.'

'Purr,' said Harriet.

'I promise. And we'll never ever tell anybody else,' Hank said, rather fiercely. 'Ever! Because – you know how people are. If people saw them—'

'I promise,' Susan said. She and Hank shook hands, promising.

Roger flew gracefully over and landed on Hank's shoulder.

'Purr,' said Roger.

'They could live in the old barn,' Susan said. 'Nobody ever goes there but us. There's that dovecote up in the loft, with all those holes in the wall where the doves flew in and out.'

'We can take hay up there and make them a place to sleep,' Hank said.

'Purr,' said Roger.

Very softly and gently Hank raised his hand and stroked Roger right between the wings.

'Oooh,' said James, watching. He jumped down off the stump and came trotting over to the children. He sat down near Susan's shoes. Very softly and gently Susan reached down and scratched James under the chin and behind the ears.

'Purr,' James said, and drooled a little on Susan's shoe.

'Oh, well!' said Thelma, having cleaned up the

last of the cold roast beef. She arose in the air, flew over with great dignity, sat right down in Hank's lap, folded her wings, and said, 'Purr, purr, purr . . .'

'Oh Hank,' Susan whispered, 'their wings are furry.'

'Oh, James,' Harriet whispered, 'their hands are kind.'

THE DAYDREAMER

by Ian McEwan

I've often wondered what it feels like to be a cat. They seem to have a very happy relaxed lifestyle – lots of eating, lots of sunbathing, lots of sleeping, and an occasional exciting hunting spree at dawn or dusk. I stare into Jacob or Lily's eyes and try hard to imagine what they're actually thinking. They look so wise and profound you'd expect them to be contemplating the secrets of the universe, but they're probably just wondering when I'm next going to feed them.

Ian McEwan has clearly wondered what it's like to be a cat himself. He's a famous literary novelist for adults, but he's written one very interesting, slightly weird book for children. His main character, Peter, is a daydreamer, and all sorts of magical things happen to him. There's a distinctly creepy chapter

about a Bad Doll with only one fat pink leg who comes alive. The following extract comes from my favourite chapter, where Peter changes places with his cat, William.

JnS

🐾 THE DAYDREAMER 🐾

When Peter snatched up his satchel, and took one last look around before running out of the house, it was always William he saw. His head was cushioned on one paw, while the other dangled carelessly over the edge of the shelf, dabbling in the rising warmth. Now the ridiculous humans were leaving, a cat could get in a few hours of serious snoozing. The image of the dozing cat tormented Peter as he stepped out of the house into the icy blast of the north wind.

If you believe it is strange to think of a cat as a real member of a family, then you should know that William's age was greater than Peter and Kate's together. As a young cat he knew their mother when she was still at school. He had gone with her to university, and five years later had been present at her wedding reception. When Viola Fortune was expecting her first baby, and rested in bed some afternoons, William Cat used to drape himself over the big round hump in her middle that was Peter. At the births of both Peter and Kate, he had disappeared from the house for days on end. No one knew where or why he went. He had quietly observed all the sorrows and joys of family life. He had watched the babies become toddlers who tried to carry him about by the ears, and he had seen the toddlers turn into school children. He had known the parents when they were a wild young couple living in one room. Now they were less wild in their three-bedroomed house. And William Cat was less wild too. He no longer brought mice or birds into the house to lay them at the feet of ungrateful humans. Soon after his fourteenth birthday he gave up fighting and no longer proudly defended his territory. Peter thought it outrageous that a bully of a young tom from next door was taking over the garden, knowing that old William could not do a thing about it. Sometimes the tom came through the cat flap into the kitchen and ate William's food while the old cat watched helplessly. And only a few years before, no sensible cat would have dared set a paw upon the lawn.

William must have been sad about the loss of his powers. He gave up the company of other cats and sat alone in the house with his memories and reflections. But despite his seventeen years, he kept himself sleek and trim. He was mostly black, with dazzling white socks and shirt front, and a splash of white in the tip of his tail. Sometimes he would seek you out where you were sitting, and after a moment's thought, jump on to your lap and stand there, feet splayed, gazing deeply without blinking into your eyes. Then he might cock his head, still holding your gaze, and miaow, just once, and you would know he was telling you something important and wise, something you would never understand.

There was nothing Peter liked better on a winter's afternoon when he came home from school than to kick off his shoes and lie down beside William Cat in front of the living-room fire. He liked to get right down to William's level, and to put his face up close to the cat's and see how extraordinary it really was, how beautifully non-human, with spikes of black hair sprouting in a globe from a tiny face beneath the fur, and the white whiskers with their slight downwards curve, and the eyebrow hairs shooting up like radio antennae, and the pale green eyes with their upright slits, like doors ajar into a world Peter could never enter. As soon as he came close to the cat, the deep rumbling purr would begin, so low and strong that the floor vibrated. Peter knew he was welcome.

It was just one such afternoon, a Tuesday as it happened, four o'clock and already the light fading, curtains drawn and lights on, when Peter eased himself on to the carpet where William lay before a bright fire whose flames were curling round a fat elm log. Down the chimney came the moan of the freezing wind as it whipped across the rooftops. Peter had sprinted from the bus stop with Kate to keep warm. Now he was safely indoors with his old friend who was pretending to be younger than his years by rolling on to his back and letting his front paws flop helplessly. He wanted his chest tickled. As Peter began to move his fingers lightly through the fur, the rumbling noise grew louder, so loud that every bone in the old cat's body rattled. And then, William stretched out a paw to Peter's fingers and tried to draw them up higher. Peter let the cat guide his hand.

'Do you want me to tickle your chin?' he murmured. But no. The cat wanted to be touched right at the base of his throat. Peter felt something hard there. It moved from side to side when he touched it. Something had got trapped in the fur. Peter propped

himself on an elbow in order to investigate. He parted
the fur. At first he thought he was looking at a piece
of jewellery, a little silver tag. But there was no chain,
and as he poked and peered he saw that it was not
metal at all, but polished bone, oval and flattened
in the centre, and most curiously of all, that it was
attached to William Cat's skin. The piece of bone fitted
well between his forefinger and thumb. He tightened
his grip and gave a tug. William Cat's purr grew even
louder. Peter pulled again, downwards, and this time
he felt something give.

Looking down through the fur, and parting it with
the tips of his fingers, he saw that he had opened
up a small slit in the cat's skin. It was as if he were
holding the handle of a zip. Again he pulled, and now
there was a dark opening two inches long. William
Cat's purr was coming from in there. Perhaps, Peter
thought, I'll see his heart beating. A paw was gently
pushing against his fingers again. William Cat wanted
him to go on.

And this is what he did. He unzipped the whole
cat from throat to tail. Peter wanted to part the skin
to peep inside. But he did not wish to appear nosy.
He was just about to call out to Kate when there was
a movement, a stirring inside the cat, and from the
opening in the fur there came a faint pink glow which

grew brighter. And suddenly, out of William Cat climbed a, well, a thing, a creature. But Peter was not certain that it was really there to touch, for it seemed to be made entirely of light. And while it did not have whiskers or a tail, or a purr, or even fur, or four legs, everything about it seemed to say 'cat'. It was the very essence of the word, the heart of the idea. It was a quiet, slinky, curvy fold of pink and purple light, and it was climbing out of the cat.

'You must be William's spirit,' Peter said aloud. 'Or are you a ghost?'

The light made no sound, but it understood. It seemed to say, without actually speaking the words, that it was both these things, and much more besides.

When it was clear of the cat, which continued to lie on its back on the carpet in front of the fire, the cat spirit drifted into the air, and floated up to Peter's shoulder where it settled. Peter was not frightened. He felt the glow of the spirit on his cheek. And then the light drifted behind his head, out of sight. He felt it touch his neck and a warm shudder ran down his back. The cat spirit took hold of something knobbly at the top of his spine and drew it down, right down his back, and as his own body opened up, he felt the cool air of the room tickle the warmth of his insides.

It was the oddest thing, to climb out of your body, just step out of it and leave it lying on the carpet like a shirt you had just taken off. Peter saw his own glow, which was purple and the purest white. The two spirits hovered in the air facing each other. And then Peter suddenly knew what he wanted to do, what he had to do. He floated towards William Cat and hovered. The body stood open, like a door, and it looked so inviting, so welcoming. He dropped down and stepped inside. How fine it was, to dress yourself as a cat. It was not squelchy, as he thought all insides must be. It was dry and warm. He lay on his back and slipped his arms into William's front legs. Then he wiggled his legs into William's back legs. His head fitted perfectly inside the cat's head. He glanced across at his own body just in time to see William Cat's spirit disappear inside.

Using his paws, Peter was able to zip himself up easily. He stood, and took a few steps. What a delight, to walk on four soft white paws. He could see his whiskers springing out from the sides of his face, and he felt his tail curling behind him. His tread was light, and his fur was like the most comfortable of old woollen jumpers. As his pleasure in being a cat grew, his heart swelled, and a tingling sensation deep in his throat became so strong that he could actually hear himself. Peter was purring. He was Peter Cat, and over there, was William Boy.

The boy stood up and stretched. Then, without a word to the cat at his feet, he skipped out of the room.

'Mum,' Peter heard his old body call out from the kitchen. 'I'm hungry. What's for supper?'

That night Peter was too restless, too excited, too much of a cat to sleep. Towards ten o'clock he slipped through the cat flap. The freezing night air could not penetrate his thick fur coat. He padded soundlessly towards the garden wall. It towered above him, but one effortless, graceful leap and he was up, surveying his territory. How wonderful to see into dark corners, to feel every vibration of the night air on his whiskers, and to make himself invisible when, at midnight, a fox came up the garden path to root among the dustbins. All around he was aware of other cats, some local, some from far away, going about their nighttime business, travelling their routes. After the fox, a young tabby had tried to enter the garden. Peter warned him off with a hiss and a flick of his tail. He had purred inwardly as the young fellow squealed in astonishment and took flight.

Not long after that, while patrolling the high wall that rose above the greenhouse, he came face to face with another cat, a more dangerous intruder. It was completely black, which was why Peter had not seen it sooner. It was the tom from next door, a vigorous fellow almost twice his size, with a thick neck and long powerful legs. Without even thinking, Peter arched his back and upended his fur to make himself look big.

'Hey puss,' he hissed, 'this is my wall and you're on it.'

The black cat looked surprised. It smiled. 'So it was your wall once, Grandad. What'ya going to do about it now?'

'Beat it, before I throw you off.' Peter was amazed at how strongly he felt. This *was* his wall, his garden, and it was his job to keep unfriendly cats out.

The black cat smiled again, coldly. 'Listen, Grandad. It hasn't been your wall for a long time. I'm coming through. Out of my way or I'll rip your fur off.'

Peter stood his ground. 'Take another step, you walking flea circus, and I'll tie your whiskers round your neck.'

The black cat gave out a long laughing wail of contempt. But it did not take another step. All around, local cats were appearing out of the darkness to watch. Peter heard their voices.

A fight?

The old boy must be crazy!

He's seventeen if he's a day.

The black cat arched its powerful spine and howled again, a terrible rising note.

Peter tried to keep his voice calm, but his words came out in a hiss. 'You don't take ssshort cutsss through here without asssking me firssst.'

The black cat blinked. The muscles in its fat neck rippled as it shrieked its laugh that was also a war cry.

On the opposite wall, a moan of excitement ran through the crowd which was still growing.

'Old Bill has flipped.'

'He's chosen the wrong cat to pick a fight with.'

'Listen, you toothless old sheep,' the black cat said through a hiss far more penetrating than Peter's. 'I'm number one round here. Isn't that right?'

The black cat half turned to the crowd which murmured its agreement. Peter thought the watching cats did not sound very enthusiastic.

'My advice to you,' the black cat went on, 'is to step aside. Or I'll spread your guts all over the lawn.'

Peter knew he had gone too far now to back down. He extended his claws to take a firm grip of the wall. 'You bloated rat! This is my wall, d'you hear. And you are nothing but the soft turd of a sick dog!'

The black cat gasped. There were titters in the crowd. Peter was always such a polite boy. How splendid it was now to spit out these insults.

'You'll be birds' breakfast,' the black cat warned, and took a step forwards. Peter snatched a deep breath. For old William's sake he had to win. Even as he was thinking this, the black cat's paw lashed out at his face. Peter had an old cat's body, but he had a young boy's mind. He ducked and felt the paw and its vicious outstretched claws go singing through the air above his ears. He had time to see how the black cat was supported momentarily on only three legs. Immediately he sprang forwards, and with his two front paws pushed the tom hard in the chest. It was not the kind of thing a cat does in a fight and the number one cat was taken by surprise. With a yelp of astonishment, he slipped and tottered backwards, tipped off the wall and fell head first through the roof of the greenhouse below. The icy air was shattered by the crash and musical tinkle of broken glass and the earthier clatter of breaking flowerpots. Then there was silence. The hushed crowd of cats peered down from their wall. They heard a movement, then a groan. Then, just visible in the gloom was the shape of the black cat hobbling across the lawn. They heard it muttering.

'It's not fair. Claws and teeth, yes. But pushing like that. It just isn't fair.'

'Next time,' Peter called down, 'you ask permission.'

The black cat did not reply, but something about its retreating, limping shape made it clear it had understood.

The next morning, Peter lay on the shelf above the radiator with his head cushioned on one paw, while the other dangled loosely in the rising warmth. All about him was hurry and chaos. Kate could not find her satchel. The porridge was burned. Mr Fortune was in a bad mood because the coffee had run out and he needed three strong cups to start his day. The kitchen was a mess and the mess was covered in porridge smoke. And it was late late late!

Peter curled his tail around his back paws and tried not to purr too loudly. On the far side of the room was his old body with William Cat inside, and that body had to go to school. William Boy was looking confused. He had his coat on and he was ready to leave, but he was wearing only one shoe. The other was nowhere to be found. 'Mum,' he kept bleating. 'Where's my shoe?' But Mrs Fortune was in the hallway arguing with someone on the phone.

Peter Cat half closed his eyes. After his victory he was desperately tired. Soon the family would be gone. The house would fall silent. When the radiator had cooled, he would wander upstairs and find the most comfortable of the beds. For old time's sake he would choose his own.

The day passed just as he had hoped. Dozing, lapping a saucer of milk, dozing again, munching through some tinned cat food that really was not as bad as it smelled – rather like shepherd's pie without the mashed potato. Then more dozing. Before he knew it, the sky outside was darkening and the children were home from school. William Boy looked worn out from a day of classroom and playground struggle. Boy-cat and cat-boy lay down together in front of the living-room fire. It was most odd, Peter Cat thought, to be stroked by a hand that only the day before had belonged to him. He wondered if William Boy was happy with his new life of school and buses, and having a sister and a mum and dad. But the boy's face told Peter Cat nothing. It was so hairless, whiskerless and pink, with eyes so round that it was impossible to know what they were saying.

Later that evening, Peter wandered up to Kate's room. As usual she was talking to her dolls, giving them a lesson in geography. From the fixed expression on their faces it was clear that they were not much interested in the longest rivers in the world. Peter jumped on to her lap and she began to tickle him absent-mindedly as she talked. If only she could have known that the creature on her lap was her brother. Peter lay down and purred. Kate was beginning to list all the capital cities she could think of. It was so exquisitely boring, just what he needed to get him off to sleep again. His eyes were already closed when the door crashed open and William Boy strode in.

'Hey Peter,' Kate said. 'You didn't knock.'

But her brother-cat paid no attention. He crossed the room, picked up her cat brother roughly and hurried away with him. Peter disliked being carried. It was undignified for a cat of his age. He tried to struggle, but William Boy only tightened his grip as he rushed down the stairs. 'Ssh,' he said. 'We don't have much time.'

William carried the cat into the living room and set him down.

'Keep still,' the boy whispered. 'Do what I tell you. Roll on to your back.'

Peter Cat had little choice for the boy had pinned him down with one hand and was searching in his fur with the other. He found the piece of polished bone and pulled downwards. Peter felt the cool air reach his insides. He stepped out of the cat's body. The boy was reaching up behind his own neck and unzipping himself. Now the pink and purple light of a true cat slipped out of the boy's body. For a moment the two spirits, cat and human, faced each other, suspended above the carpet. Below them, their bodies lay still, waiting, like taxis ready to move off with their passengers. There was a sadness in the air.

Though the cat spirit did not speak, Peter sensed what it was saying. 'I must return,' it said. 'I have another adventure to begin. Thank you for letting me be a boy. I have learned so many things that will be useful to me in the time to come. But most of all, thank you for fighting my last battle for me.'

Peter was about to speak, but the cat spirit was returning to its own body.

'There's very little time,' it seemed to say, as the pink and purple light folded itself into the fur of the cat. Peter drifted towards his own body, and slipped in round the back, at the top of the spine.

It felt rather odd at first. This body did not really fit him. When he stood up he was shaky on his legs. It was like wearing a pair of gumboots four sizes too large. Perhaps his body had grown a little since he had last used it. It felt safer to lie down for the moment. As he did so the cat, William Cat, turned and walked very slowly and stiffly out of the room without even a glance at him.

As Peter lay there, trying to get used to his old body, he noticed a curious thing. The fire was still curling round the same elm log. He glanced towards the window. The sky was darkening. It was not evening, it was still late afternoon. From the newspaper lying near a chair, he could see that it was still Tuesday. And here was another curious thing. His sister Kate was running into the room crying. And following her were his parents, looking very grim.

'Oh Peter,' his sister cried. 'Something terrible has happened.'

'It's William Cat,' his mother explained. 'I'm afraid he's . . .'

'Oh William!' Kate's wail drowned her mother's words.

'He just walked into the kitchen,' his father said, 'and climbed on to his favourite shelf above the radiator, closed his eyes and . . . died.'

'He didn't feel a thing,' Viola Fortune said reassuringly.

Kate continued to cry. Peter realized that his parents were watching him anxiously, waiting to see how he was going to take the news. Of all the family, he was the one who had been closest to the cat.

'He was seventeen,' Thomas Fortune said. 'He had a good innings.'

'He had a good life,' Viola Fortune said.

Peter stood up slowly. Two legs did not seem enough.

'Yes,' he said at last. 'He's gone on another adventure now.'

The next morning they buried William at the bottom of the garden. Peter made a cross out of sticks, and Kate made a wreath out of laurel leaves and twigs. Even though they were all going to be late for school or work, the whole family went down to the graveside together. The children put on the final shovelfuls of earth. And it was just then that there rose through the ground and hovered in the air a shining ball of pink and purple light.

'Look!' Peter said, and pointed.

'Look at what?'

'Right there, right in front of you.'

'Peter, what are you talking about?'

'He's daydreaming again.'

The light drifted higher until it was level with Peter's head. It did not speak, of course. That would have been impossible. But Peter heard it all the same.

'Goodbye, Peter,' it said as it began to fade before his eyes. 'Goodbye, and thanks again.'

ICE LOLLY

by Jean Ure

I've been friends with Jean Ure for many years, so we often send each other our books when they're newly published. I think my absolute favourite is Ice Lolly. *It's probably not surprising that I'm so fond of Laurel, the main girl in the story, because she loves books and cats more than anything else, and so do I!*

Ice Lolly *is quite a sad story, because Laurel's special mum has died and she has to go and live with her aunt and uncle and their children. With her she takes boxes of her mum's books, and Mr Pooter, her beloved cat. Auntie Ellen is very houseproud and particular. Nearly all the books are put up in the attic – and poor Mr Pooter is barely tolerated.*

I think you'll enjoy the following extract, and don't worry – if you read the whole book you'll find there's a wonderful happy ending.

JꝡS

😻 ICE LOLLY 😻

Today in the library Mrs Caton gives me a book to read in the holidays. It's called *Three Men in a Boat*, and it's old. I like old books! I like the thought of other people reading them. People from long ago, before I was born. I imagine them turning the pages and chuckling to themselves at bits they find amusing, or maybe going *tut* if there's something they don't approve of, and never dreaming that years later, in another century, someone like me will be turning those same pages and reading the exact same words.

I put the book to my nose and sniff. I always do this with books; Mum used to do it, too. She used to say that the smell of a book was better than the smell of the most expensive perfume.

Mrs Caton laughs. 'Why is it that real book people always do that?' she says.

'Do what?' says Jolene, jealously. She likes to think of herself as a book person, in spite of not knowing whether Elinor M. Brent-Dyer goes under B or D. I bet she couldn't get through *Jane Eyre*, even though she is in Year Nine. I read it with Mum when I was only ten!

Now I am being boastful. *I have nothing to be boastful about*. Yesterday we had the results of our end-of-term maths exam, and I came next to bottom. On the other hand, I came top of English. Mum would have been ever so proud. She would have said, 'You take after me, Lollipop, you don't have a mathematical brain. You're more of a language person.'

But coming next to bottom is nothing to boast about; even Mum would agree with that. So I have absolutely no right to feel superior to Jolene. She might have come *top* of her maths exam, for all I know.

I tell her about books smelling better than perfume, and she does that thing that people are always doing, she looks at me like I'm from outer space.

'Dalek!' she hisses, as she flounces off across the library.

'What did she call you?' says Mrs Caton.

I mutter, 'Dalek,' hoping that she won't hear and will just forget about it. But she's frowning.

'Why Dalek?' she says.

I say that I don't know.

'It doesn't seem a very pleasant thing to call someone.'

I tell her that it's like a sort of nickname. Nickname makes it sound friendly. Mrs Caton doesn't look like she's convinced. She says, 'Well, anyway, I was going through my bookshelves and I came across *Three Men in a Boat* and I thought of you immediately. It was written round about the same time as your favourite, *Diary of a Nobody*. My dad introduced me to it. I used to think it was absolutely hilarious! Mind you, that was when I was about fifteen or sixteen, so I was quite a bit older than you. But you're such a mature reader . . . I'll be interested to know how you get on. Give it a go and see what you feel.'

I promise her that I will.

'You can read it over the summer holiday. Just a little bit at a time.'

Earnestly, I say that I never read books a little bit at a time. 'Once I've started I can't stop. I just get greedy and gobble them up!'

'Well, don't get too greedy,' says Mrs Caton.

'You've got weeks and weeks ahead of you.'

The bell rings for the start of afternoon school. Tomorrow is the last day of term. I tell Mrs Caton a big thank you.

'I'll start reading straight away! And I'll take really good care of it.'

'I know you will,' she says. 'You're a book person. But don't forget . . . a little bit at a time. I don't want you being bored.'

I couldn't be bored by a *book*. I tell her this, and she smiles and says, 'Different books suit different people . . . and don't gobble! You've got the whole of the summer.'

I go slowly back to class. I can't imagine what I'm going to do all through the summer. I can't imagine not going to the library every day and seeing Mrs Caton. I don't think, really, that I'm looking forward to all those empty weeks.

I used to love the holidays when Mum was here. We never went away anywhere, we couldn't afford it, but we used to go on days out. We used to visit places, all over London. Sometimes out of London, like we'd jump on the train and go to the seaside and buy sticks of rock and paddle and build sandcastles. It was fun! Even if we just packed sandwiches and went to Kensington Gardens to see Peter Pan and feed the ducks. Or like maybe Mum would suddenly say, 'Let's go somewhere different! Let's catch a train and just go off . . . where shall we go to? Tell me which direction! North, east, south, west . . . you choose!'

So then I'd say, like, 'North!' and off we'd go to King's Cross or Euston. We'd look at the indicator boards and Mum would say, 'Pick a destination!' I knew I couldn't pick anywhere too far away, like Birmingham or Manchester, but it still gave us lots to choose from.

We didn't really go places so much after Mum was in her wheelchair, but we still had fun. We'd stay home and play games, like Scrabble, or Trivial Pursuit, or Monopoly. We didn't have a Monopoly board, but Mum said that needn't stop us, we'd make one for ourselves. Making the board was almost as much fun as playing the game! We printed out lots of money on the computer and Mum giggled and said, 'Let's hope the police don't break in and catch us at it! They'll think we're forgers.'

I bet if the police *had* broken in, it would still have been fun. Everything was fun, with Mum. It's not much fun with Uncle Mark and Auntie Ellen. They never play games, and if I suggested going to the station and choosing a place to visit they'd give me that look, like, *How weird is that child?*

They're going to Wales in August. I suppose I'll go with them, though I don't know where I'll stay. Holly and Michael are staying with their nan, but there isn't room for anyone else so Uncle Mark and Auntie Ellen are booked into a hotel. I don't think Auntie Ellen would want to pay for me to be booked in as well, she's already complaining about how much it costs. So I don't know quite what will happen. Maybe I could go and stay with Stevie, except that Stevie doesn't have people to stay. Perhaps I'll just stay behind, by myself. That would probably be best, otherwise what would happen to Mr Pooter? He couldn't come to Wales, and Auntie Ellen wouldn't pay for a cattery, and anyway he would *hate* being in a cattery. But I'm not leaving him home alone!

When I get back after school I find him curled up on the bed. He chirrups at me, but doesn't get up. I look quickly round to check that he hasn't had any more accidents. Yesterday he was sick on the duvet; just a little bit, I managed to sponge it off. Today I can't see anything. My heart lifts.

'Good boy,' I say. 'Good boy!' I scratch behind his ears, the way he likes, and try to roll him over to tickle his tummy, but he won't roll. 'OK, dinner time,' I say. I fetch his bowl and one of his new expensive cat food tins. In the old days he was so eager that he used to jump up and head-butt, and push his way into the bowl before Mum had even had a chance to get the food in there. He doesn't do that, now. I have to coax him.

I take his bowl over to the bed. He doesn't look at it.

'Nice kitty food,' I say. 'Yum yum!' I pick up the bowl and pretend to eat out of it myself. Mr Pooter watches me, unblinking. 'Now you have some!' I offer him the bowl again, but he turns his head away. 'Chicken and liver . . . yummy yummy!' I smear a bit on my finger. His blunt nose crimples. He's almost tempted . . . and then he turns away again. He's not going to eat, no matter how hard I try.

I sit on the bed, stroking him. Stevie once said that cats are creatures of habit. 'They don't like change. Upsets them.' I think that maybe Mr Pooter is missing Mum. I whisper, 'I miss her, too!' I wish there was something I could do to make him happy. I wish he could creep into my ice house with me. We could huddle there together, and no one could get at us.

I go down to tea, leaving his bowl beside him on the bed. When I come back, it is still there; the food is still in it. I'm beginning to worry. His coat isn't as shiny as it used to be, and I can feel his ribs sticking out. I don't know what to do!

I'm going to ring Stevie; Stevie will know. She knows everything about cats. I take my mobile out of my bag and bring up her number. My heart is thumping. As a rule, in the evening, she doesn't bother to answer. She and Mum had a special code. Mum would let the phone ring three times, then immediately ring again, so that Stevie would know it was her. But I'm not sure she'll remember; her memory isn't what it was. And even if she does, she still mightn't answer. She'll know it can't be Mum.

If she does answer, she'll be cross. She hates people telephoning her. But I have to do it, for Mr Pooter.

I let the phone ring three times and press the off button. Then I ring again, and this time I let it keep ringing. It rings and it rings. I sink down next to Mr Pooter, and for just a minute my ice house begins to crumble. I feel the back of my eyes prickling. And then I hear Stevie's voice, barking into my ear.

'*Yes?*'

'S-Stevie?' I say.

'Who is this?'

She sounds suspicious. I tell her that it's Laurel. She says, 'Laurel Winton? This time of night?'

It's only six o'clock but Stevie is an old lady. I stammer that I'm really sorry to be a nuisance.

'Well, get on with it,' says Stevie. 'I'm in the middle of feeding time.' And then she shouts, very loudly, 'You! Thomas. Get out of that dish!'

I giggle, in spite of myself. She has always had trouble with Thomas. He's large and stripy and he steals food.

'No laughing matter,' grumbles Stevie. 'Cat has no morality. What can I do for you?'

I tell her that I'm worried about Mr Pooter. 'He doesn't want to eat and he keeps being sick and his ribs are showing!'

'Kidneys,' says Stevie.

I swallow. 'Is that serious?'

'Old cat. Could be. Needs to go to the vet. Get treated.'

'Will they be able to make him better?'

Stevie says there are things that can be done. Special diets. Tablets. But I must take him straight away. 'No hanging around. Get him there immediately.'

I falter. 'You mean, like . . . now?'

'Tomorrow. Make an appointment.'

I hear myself wailing down the phone, 'I don't know where the vet is!'

'Yellow Pages,' snaps Stevie. 'Local library. Ask!' And then, in her gruff, gravelly voice, she goes, 'Must look after him. Gave your mum a lot of pleasure. Not fair to let him suffer.'

I wouldn't! I wouldn't ever let Mr Pooter suffer. I tell Stevie that I will do what she says. I will find a vet and I will make an appointment.

Talking to Stevie makes me feel strong and confident. I can do what she says. I *will* do what she says. It's for Mr Pooter.

And then I ring off, and bit by bit my confidence starts to trickle away. Instead of feeling strong I feel feeble and useless. I'm not sure that someone of twelve years old *can* make appointments with vets. And even if they can, how am I going to pay? Vets cost money. I don't know how much, but a lot more than my pocket money. What am I going to do?

I look at Mr Pooter, trustfully gazing up at me from the bed, and I know that I have to do *something*. I wish Mum was here! But she isn't. It's up to me. I know what I have to do, I have to get my courage up and ask Uncle Mark.

I go downstairs. Uncle Mark is in his shed. He makes things in there, bird tables and dolls' houses and stuff, which he sells to people. Mum always said he should have been a carpenter instead of the manager of a DIY shop.

I tell him that Mr Pooter needs to go to the vet. 'He's

not eating properly. I think it might be his kidneys.'

'Well, now, Lol, you have to face it,' says Uncle Mark, 'he is an old cat. I'm not quite sure how much they can do.'

'There's tablets,' I say. 'They can make him better. *Please!* Can't we make an appointment?'

For a minute I think he's going to say no; but then he sighs and says all right, we'll take him along. 'I'll ask next door, they've got a cat. They'll know which the nearest vet is.'

I settle down to do my homework, with Mr Pooter sitting next to me. I tell him that we're going to take him to the doctor and get some medicine. I feel happier now that I've talked to Uncle Mark. But then I go downstairs to get a glass of milk and Uncle Mark and Auntie Ellen are in the kitchen and the door is open a crack so that I can hear their voices. I hear Auntie Ellen saying something about 'Ridiculous expense' and Uncle Mark saying 'All she's got', and I know that they're talking about me and Mr Pooter. I turn, and come rushing back upstairs and into my room, where I fling myself on to the bed and cuddle Mr Pooter as hard as ever I can.

'I love you, I love you, I love you,' I whisper, into his fur. Mr Pooter rubs his head against me, and I tell him that everything is going to be all right. I'll look after him.

I decide that I will make a start on *Three Men in a Boat*. It is about these three men who go off in a boat with a dog called Montmorency. I know that it is supposed to be funny because of Mrs Caton telling me how she found it hilarious, so I am trying to find bits that make me laugh. When I find one I am going to write it down in my special notebook that Mum gave me last Christmas. It has a beautiful silk cover, embroidered in bright blues and oranges and emerald greens, with scarlet flowers. I have the page already open, but so far I haven't found anything. It is quite worrying as I am already on page 32. I have to find *something* funny so that I can tell Mrs Caton tomorrow. She would be disappointed if I don't like her book.

There's a bit about Montmorency, saying how his idea of living is to collect a gang of the most disreputable dogs he can find and lead them round town to fight other disreputable dogs. And a bit where J, who is the man telling the story, can't find his coat and grows very cross when none of his friends can find it, either. He says, 'You might just as well ask the cat to find anything!' Those bits are quite funny, I suppose. Especially the cat bit. I remember once when Mum had lost the front door key and we were looking all over for it, and Mr Pooter just sat there, with his paws tucked in, watching as we crawled round the room on our hands and knees, peering under the sofa and poking down the sides of chairs. And then he yawned, and stood up, and we discovered that he'd been sitting on it the whole time. Sitting on the front door key! Mum said, 'That is just so typical of a cat!'

I am about to take out my pen and start writing things down, to tell Mrs Caton, when Michael knocks at the door and says, 'Dad wants you to come downstairs and be with the rest of us.' I hesitate. 'You're part of the family,' says Michael. 'You can't keep hiding away.'

Reluctantly, I put down my notebook. Michael looks at me. He seems concerned. He says, 'Don't you like being with us?'

I feel my cheeks grow pink. I mumble that I don't think Auntie Ellen really wants me here. It's not a criticism! If this was my house, I probably wouldn't want me here.

Now I've made Michael's cheeks go pink as well. He says that Auntie Ellen is doing her best to make me feel welcome. 'She wants you to be happy . . . I think you should come down.'

I leave Mr Pooter curled up on the duvet and obediently go with Michael to join the rest of the family. Holly, very self-important, informs me that Auntie

Ellen has just finished making her costume for Book Week. 'I'm going as a Woodland Fairy . . . *Holly tree* fairy! Can I try it on, Mum?'

She puts it on and starts pirouetting round the room.

'Yuck,' says Michael; but he's not being fair. Auntie Ellen is good at sewing. She's made this really brilliant costume, all decorated with shiny green leaves and bright red berries.

'Did you ever dress up for Book Week?' says Holly. 'What did you dress up as?'

'A pirate,' I say.

'A *pirate*? You don't have girl pirates!'

'Why not?' says Michael.

''Cos you don't! Why did you go as a pirate?'

'Just fancied it,' I say.

I didn't really fancy it. I wanted to go as a fairy. Rainbow Fairy. That's what I'd set my heart on. But Mum wasn't ever very good at sewing. My fairy skirt was all limp and saggy, and the top bit didn't fit properly. And when I picked up my fairy wand it immediately collapsed, which made Mum giggle. I didn't giggle; I burst into tears. I sobbed and raged, 'cos now what was I going to do?

'I look like I'm wearing a dish rag!' I blamed Mum for leaving everything till the last minute. 'Like you always do! Everyone else has had their costumes for weeks.'

Mum immediately stopped giggling and promised that she would make me something else. 'Something better! Even if I have to sit up all night.' Which she did. She made me this pirate outfit and I wasn't in the least bit grateful. I shouted that I didn't want to be a pirate, I wanted to be a Rainbow Fairy. Poor Mum! She begged me to give her a kiss and say she was for-given, but I wouldn't. I went off in a sulk and spent the whole day being jealous of all the people who had proper mums, who made them lovely sparkly fairy dresses which didn't sag and bag. I was still cross when I got home. Mum tried so hard to make it up to me.

'Oh, Lollipop, I'm so sorry,' she said. 'I'm such a rotten mum!'

But she wasn't. She wasn't! She was the best mum anyone ever had. I wish so much that I'd told her so!

I have to go back upstairs. I need to cuddle Mr Pooter.

'Where are you off to?' says Auntie Ellen. 'You've only just come down.'

I tell her that I have to write a book report for Mrs Caton. 'I want to do it while it's fresh in my mind.' Auntie Ellen shakes her head, like, *I give up!*

'Go on, then,' she says. 'If that's what you want.'

I gallop back up the stairs. Mr Pooter opens an eye and stretches. I check the room, but I don't think he's moved, so that is all right.

'Good boy,' I say. 'Good boy!'

I settle down beside him and start writing in my notebook. I put down the bit about Montmorency and his gang of dogs. I put down the cat bit. I can't think of anything else. The truth is, I am finding this book quite difficult to get into. Maybe it is because I am worried about Mr Pooter and not in the right mood. Or maybe it's because this is the first grown-up book that I have tried to read on my own, without Mum. If Mum were reading it to me, and doing all the voices, then I am sure I would find lots to laugh at. But I am not going to give up! I am a real book person and Mrs Caton is eagerly waiting to know how I get on.

On the way in to school this morning Uncle Mark says that he will ring the vet and make an appointment for this evening. Auntie Ellen is with us, as it is one of her days when she works in the shop. She says that she is the one who will be coming with me. My heart goes plummeting. I don't want Auntie Ellen coming with me! But I haven't any choice. It's Thursday, and late-night shopping, and Uncle Mark won't be home in time.

After lunch I go to the library. I take out my note-book and read Mrs Caton the bits I've written down.

'I think those bits were hilarious,' I say.

I wasn't quite sure what the word hilarious meant until I looked it up in the dictionary. It means 'very funny', and I didn't honestly find either of the bits *very* funny. Just a little bit funny. But Mrs Caton looks pleased.

'I'm so glad you're enjoying it,' she says. 'I thought you would.'

I promise her that I will make a note of all the other bits I find funny, so that I can tell her about them. She says that's a good idea.

'It'll be something to look forward to at the start of next term.'

'I'll have finished it long before then,' I say. 'I'll probably have read a million others by then!'

Now I'm being boastful again. I don't mean to be, but it's probably true. I will have read a million others. There are eight long weeks to go and I can't think what else there'll be to do.

I get home to find Auntie Ellen waiting impatiently for me. 'Go and fetch the cat,' she says. 'Put it in its box, we have to be at the vet for 4.15.'

I hate that she calls Mr Pooter 'the cat'. He's Mr Pooter! I go upstairs to get him and he purrs amiably.

I think he quite likes his box. Holly, for some reason, insists on coming with us. She says she's never been to the vet's before and she wants to know what it's like. I tell her it's like being at the doctor's, except all the patients are animals.

We sit in the Reception area, waiting to be called. I hold Mr Pooter on my lap, in his box. He crouches, watchfully. There are other people with cats, some people with dogs, one little girl with a pet rabbit. I try to interest Mr Pooter in the rabbit, but Auntie Ellen tells me sharply not to make a nuisance of myself. All I was doing was just turning his box in the right direction, so he could see! Holly wrinkles her nose and says there's a smell. Auntie Ellen tells her it's disinfectant and she goes, 'Ugh! Yuck! Poo!' But then a vet puts his head round the door and calls out, 'Fluffy Marshall?' and Holly giggles – *'Fluffy Marshall!'* – and wants to know whether that's the name of the cat or the name of the owner. Auntie Ellen tells her to be quiet and stop showing off, so then she sits in a sulk, scuffing her feet on the floor.

When it's our turn the vet calls, 'Pooter Walters!' He's not Pooter Walters, he's Pooter Winton, but I suppose it's not really important. What's important is that the vet is going to make him better.

We all troop into the surgery. The vet asks what the problem seems to be, and I tell him about Mr Pooter being sick and not wanting to eat.

'And how old is he?' says the vet.

Proudly I say that he's sixteen.

'Quite an old fellow,' says the vet.

He examines Mr Pooter all over. Mr Pooter is so good! He doesn't complain once. I stroke him and tell him that everything is going to be all right.

'Well,' says the vet, straightening up. 'In view of his age, I'd say it's almost certainly a kidney problem, but we'd better do a blood test to make sure.'

'Is that really necessary?' says Auntie Ellen.

The vet says if we want a proper diagnosis, it is.

'What I mean,' says Auntie Ellen, 'is it really worth it? At his age?'

I hold my breath. I squeeze Mr Pooter.

'We can't treat him if we don't know what's wrong,' says the vet. 'I agree that he's old, but he's not ancient. Cats can easily live to be nineteen or twenty. Even older.'

I am so relieved I let out my breath in a big *whoosh*. I don't think Auntie Ellen is too happy, but she lets the vet take a sample of Mr Pooter's blood. I keep him very close and whisper in his ear and he doesn't even flinch. He is a very brave cat. The vet says the results will be through in a couple of days and then we can decide on the appropriate treatment. In the meanwhile, he says, we should try him with a special diet.

I put Mr Pooter back in his box and we go out to Reception to collect some cans of special cat diet and pay the bill. I am scared when I see how much the bill comes to. I would have to save up my pocket money for months before I would have enough to pay it. Auntie Ellen is outraged. Angrily she drives us home, saying over and over that it is daylight robbery. I tell her that I will pay it back, that Uncle Mark needn't give me any more pocket money until—

'Until kingdom come!' snaps Auntie Ellen. 'Don't be absurd.'

'It's her cat,' says Holly, 'so she *ought* to pay it back.'

I say that I will. 'I promise!'

'It's only fair,' says Holly.

Auntie Ellen tells us both to be quiet. 'I've had enough for one day.'

As soon as we're back I go upstairs with Mr Pooter and ring Stevie. It's only five o'clock, so maybe she won't be too cross. She's not cross at all! She wants to hear about Mr Pooter. I tell her what the vet said and she says that the special diet will help, but if Mr

Pooter is still being picky I could try buying some prawns and whizzing them up in the food processor.

'Make them into a nice soft mush . . . that should tempt him.'

I am going to go out first thing tomorrow and buy some prawns with what is left of my pocket money. Before I stop getting pocket money. I am not sure whether Uncle Mark is going to go on giving me any or not. When he came in I told him he needn't. 'I'm going to pay back every penny!' Uncle Mark told me not to be silly. He said of course I didn't need to pay him back. But then Holly chimed in with 'It's her cat!' and Auntie Ellen said again about daylight robbery. So now I don't really know. That's why I am going to buy the prawns, quickly, while I still can.

THE THEATER CAT

by Noel Streatfeild

I haven't spelled the word 'theatre' wrongly! Noel Streatfeild was a very popular English author who wrote many wonderful family stories – but she occasionally wrote for the American market too. I'm particularly fond of this sweet picture book The Theater Cat *about a delicate little cat called Pinkie who's paid fifty cents a week to catch the mice in the Ballet Theater (that's the way Americans spell it). Pinkie is pretty hopeless at his job because he's afraid of mice, but he adores the ballet – and his knowledge and expertise prove especially useful.*

It's a bizarre little story, but somehow very touching – and especially comforting if you feel a bit of an odd one out.

JﬡS

❧ THE THEATER CAT ❧

Pinkie was a slim, exquisite black cat. His tastes were elegant and he took great pride in his looks and was often to be seen peeping in mirrors, to be sure his face was clean and his whiskers tidy. He was a persnickety eater, leaving on his plate any scrap of food which seemed to him coarse or badly cooked. When offered ice cream he would accept a portion only if it were pink; and that was the reason he was christened Pinkie.

By profession Pinkie was a mouser. He was employed as a mouse catcher by the Ballet Theater. Every Friday night when the artists were paid, there was an envelope for Pinkie with his salary of

fifty cents inside; but every Friday Pinkie trembled
when he opened his envelope, in case, as well as his
salary, there should be a slip of paper saying he was
dismissed. For the dreadful truth was, Pinkie was a
failure. Everybody in the theater knew it and everybody spoke about it.

The doorkeeper said, 'That Pinkie ain't worth a
nickel. He's paid to catch mice, but I have to get 'em.
Thinks himself too highfalutin'. If I were boss around
here, I wouldn't keep him another day.'

'You could not be more right,' the wardrobe mistress agreed. 'But what can you expect from a delicate
type like that?'

The ice-cream girl thought she understood. 'Can't
really blame the cat. Pinkie's the right name for him,
seeing he only eats pink ice cream, but that's no name
for a working cat; kinda gives him ideas. Better if he
was called George.'

Every week as he fixed the pay envelopes the manager muttered, 'Have to get rid of Pinkie. What does
he think I'm paying him for? He just sits and watches
the dancers. Never knows what a mouse looks like.'

It's a fearful thing to know you are in a career for
which you are not fitted, and Pinkie knew just that.
The reason he did not make the grade was a shocking
one. *He was afraid of mice*. But he was sticking to his

job as long as it would stick to him, for even greater than his fear of mice was his love of the ballet.

Every ballet the company danced Pinkie knew, which was natural for he never missed a rehearsal or a performance. He would stand in the wings, swaying softly with the dancers, or shuddering from the final hairs on the tips of his ears to the end of his delicately tapering tail at a clumsy pirouette or an awkward lift. The dancers knew what a critic Pinkie was and one would say to the other, 'The ballet even went over with Pinkie, so we must have been good.'

It was at the final dress rehearsal of a new ballet that Pinkie was publicly shamed. It was a lovely ballet; Pinkie's eyes glistened with ecstasy. 'Beautiful!' he purred. 'Superb!' 'What a line!' Then it happened. The leading ballerina was about to spring across the stage into her cavalier's arms, when a mouse ran across her feet. She screamed. She fell. She sprained her ankle. The mouse ran. The company ran. Pinkie ran. In fact, Pinkie ran faster and farther from the mouse than anybody else.

When the ballerina had been carried to her dressing room and order restored, the manager, his face black as thunder, came onto the stage. 'Where's Pinkie?'

Pinkie, trying to look more like a black shadow than

a cat, crawled to his feet. The manager was so angry his voice wobbled. 'No star! A new ballet opening this evening! If the show flops, who is to blame? You! The theater mouser who ran when he saw a mouse! You're fired! The cashier will pay you off after the show.'

Pinkie lay at the side of the darkened stage sobbing his heart out. Fired! The news that he was a failure would be known in every theater. The mouser who ran at the sight of a mouse! What a coward! Better be dead than labeled that way. What future was there for a cat with such a reputation? What was he to do? How could he live if he never saw another ballet? How could he see a ballet unless he worked in a ballet theater? He would never earn enough to buy a seat. Never watch another ballet! Never! Never! Never! As this dreadful knowledge sank in, Pinkie cried more and more, until it was as if he were drowning in his tears.

Suddenly he caught his breath. 'Hic-cup, boo. Hic-cup, boo.' Somebody else was crying, too. Swallowing back his tears, Pinkie tiptoed across the stage. Lying under a piece of scenery was a girl of twelve, the principal ballerina's understudy. Words tumbled out of her with her tears.

'This was my big chance . . . the break I've been

waiting for . . . but I've never had a rehearsal . . . I don't know the steps well enough . . . I'll never make good now . . . I can't dance if I don't know the steps . . .'

Pinkie's heart under his shining black shirt front was swollen with pity. The understudy was underrehearsed. Here was her opportunity to become famous, and she would miss it because she had not practiced the steps. Then a thought flew to him, and happiness flowed through him. He began to purr. Who had given this little ballerina her chance? Pinkie the no-good cowardly cat. It was up to him to see she did not fail. Pinkie tapped the dancer with a paw. His paw was so soft and his tap so gentle and the dancer was crying so much that he found it hard to attract her attention, but at last she raised her head and looked at him. The moment her eyes were on him, he sprang into the air and raised himself on the toes of his hind legs. His front paws he held delicately curved above his head. The dancer recognized the pose for her first entrance. She scrambled to her feet, swallowed her tears, and stood behind Pinkie. She raised herself onto her points and lifted her arms. Softly as a little cloud, moving as delicately as a flower petal stirred by a breeze, Pinkie started to dance.

The rehearsal lasted for more than an hour. Finally the curtain rose. The performance of the new ballet started. There was never an evening like it. When the performance was over, the audience shouted and clapped. The company curtsied and bowed. The understudy took curtain calls alone, with the company, and with the conductor, but the audience would not let her go. 'Speech!' they called. 'Speech!' She took a deep breath, and stepped forward.

'Thank you for your kindness. But if I have danced well tonight, you shouldn't clap for me, but for the great master who coached me at the last minute. Are you there, Pinkie?'

Pinkie, blinking in the dazzle of lights, walked onto the stage. The conductor held one of his paws, the understudy the other. The audience rose to its feet.

'Pinkie! Pinkie! Three cheers for Pinkie! Pinkie the ballet-dancing cat!'

THROUGH THE LOOKING-GLASS

by Lewis Carroll

I expect you know the story of the two Alice books, even if you've never read them. Alice in Wonderland *and the sequel,* Through the Looking-Glass, *are the most famous classics of children's literature. There have been countless adaptations on stage and screen. Maybe you've seen Tim Burton's 3D version or the Disney cartoon. There's even an episode of my* Dumping Ground *where Jodie becomes Alice and all her friends turn into crazy Lewis Carroll characters.*

Both books are the most extraordinary original fantasies – but I remember feeling disconcerted by the stories as a child. I felt I could take only so much delightful nonsense. Reading the Alice books felt a

little like being tickled mercilessly. However, I loved the beginnings and endings of both stories – especially the start of Looking-Glass *where Alice is playing with her black kitten.*

JWS

❖ THROUGH THE ❖ LOOKING-GLASS

One thing was certain, that the *white* kitten had had nothing to do with it — it was the black kitten's fault entirely. For the white kitten had been having its face washed by the old cat for the last quarter of an hour (and bearing it pretty well, considering); so you see that it *couldn't* have had any hand in the mischief.

The way Dinah washed her children's faces was this: first she held the poor thing down by its ear with one paw, and then with the other paw she rubbed its face all over, the wrong way, beginning at the nose: and just now, as I said, she was hard at work on the white kitten, which was lying quite still and trying to purr – no doubt feeling that it was all meant for its good.

But the black kitten had been finished with earlier in the afternoon, and so, while Alice was sitting curled up in a corner of the great armchair, half talking to herself and half asleep, the kitten had been having a grand game of romps with the ball of worsted Alice had been trying to wind up, and had been rolling it up and down till it had all come undone again; and there it was, spread over the hearth-rug, all knots and tangles, with the kitten running after its own tail in the middle.

'Oh, you wicked wicked little thing!' cried Alice, catching up the kitten, and giving it a little kiss to make it understand that it was in disgrace. 'Really, Dinah ought to have taught you better manners! You *ought*, Dinah, you know you ought!' she added, looking reproachfully at the old cat, and speaking in as cross a voice as she could manage – and then she scrambled back into the armchair, taking the kitten and the worsted with her, and began winding up the ball again. But she didn't get on very fast, as she was talking all the time, sometimes to the kitten, and sometimes to herself. Kitty sat very demurely on her knee, pretending to watch the progress of the winding, and now and then putting out one paw and gently touching the ball, as if it would be glad to help if it might.

'Do you know what tomorrow is, Kitty?' Alice began. 'You'd have guessed it if you'd been up in the window with me – only Dinah was making you tidy, so you couldn't. I was watching the boys getting in sticks for the bonfire – and it wants plenty of sticks, Kitty! Only it got so cold, and it snowed, so they had to leave off. Never mind, Kitty, we'll go and see the bonfire tomorrow.' Here Alice wound two or three turns of the worsted round the kitten's neck, just to see how it would look: this led to a scramble, in which the ball rolled down upon the floor, and yards and yards of it got unwound again.

'Do you know, I was so angry, Kitty,' Alice went on, as soon as they were comfortably settled again, 'when I saw all the mischief you had been doing. I was very nearly opening the window, and putting you out into the snow! And you'd have deserved it, you little mischievous darling! What have you got to say for yourself? Now don't interrupt me!' she went on, holding up one finger. 'I'm going to tell you all your faults. Number one: you squeaked twice while Dinah was washing your face this morning. Now you can't deny it, Kitty, I heard you! What's that you say?' (pretending that the kitten was speaking.) 'Her paw went into your eye? Well, that's *your* fault, for keeping your eyes open – if you'd shut them tight up, it wouldn't have happened. Now don't make any more excuses, but listen! Number two: you pulled Snowdrop away by the tail just as I had put down the saucer of milk before her! What, you were thirsty, were you? How do you know she wasn't thirsty too? Now for number three: you unwound every bit of the worsted while I wasn't looking!

'That's three faults, Kitty, and you've not been punished for any of them yet. You know I'm saving up all your punishments for Wednesday week – suppose they had saved up all *my* punishments!' she went on, talking more to herself than the kitten. 'What *would* they do at the end of a year? I should be sent to prison, I suppose, when the day came. Or – let me see – suppose each punishment was to be going without a dinner: then, when the miserable day came, I should have to go without fifty dinners at once! Well, I shouldn't mind *that* much! I'd far rather go without them than eat them!

'Do you hear the snow against the window panes, Kitty? How nice and soft it sounds! Just as if someone was kissing the window all over outside. I wonder if the snow *loves* the trees and fields, that it kisses them so gently? And then it covers them up snug, you know, with a white quilt; and perhaps it says "Go to sleep, darlings, till the summer comes again." And when they wake up in the summer, Kitty, they dress themselves all in green, and dance about – whenever the wind blows – oh, that's very pretty!' cried Alice, dropping the ball of worsted to clap her hands. 'And I do so *wish* it was true! I'm sure the woods look sleepy in the autumn, when the leaves are getting brown.

'Kitty, can you play chess? Now, don't smile, my dear, I'm asking it seriously. Because, when we were playing just now, you watched just as if you understood it: and when I said "Check!" you purred! Well, it *was* a nice check, Kitty, and really I might have won, if it hadn't been for that nasty Knight, that came wriggling down among my pieces. Kitty, dear, let's pretend—' And here I wish I could tell you half the things Alice used to say, beginning with her favourite phrase 'Let's pretend.' She had had quite a long argument with her sister only the day before – all because Alice had begun with 'Let's pretend we're kings and queens'; and her sister, who liked being very exact, had argued that they couldn't because there were only two of them, and Alice had been reduced at last to say 'Well, *you* can be one of them then, and *I'll* be all the rest.' And once she had really frightened her old nurse by shouting suddenly in her ear, 'Nurse! Do let's pretend that I'm a hungry hyena, and you're a bone!'

But this is taking us away from Alice's speech to the kitten. 'Let's pretend that you're the Red Queen, Kitty! Do you know, I think, if you sat up and folded your arms, you'd look exactly like her. Now do try, there's a dear!' And Alice got the Red Queen off the table, and set it up before the kitten as a model for it to imitate: however, the thing didn't succeed, principally, Alice said, because the kitten wouldn't fold its arms properly. So, to punish it, she held it up to the Looking-glass, that it might see how sulky it was. '– and if you're not good directly,' she added, 'I'll put you through into Looking-glass House. How would you like *that*?

'Now, if you'll only attend, Kitty, and not talk so much, I'll tell you all my ideas about Looking-glass House. First, there's the room you can see through the glass – that's just the same as our drawing-room, only the things go the other way. I can see all of it when I get upon a chair – all but the bit just behind the fire-place. Oh! I do so wish I could see *that* bit! I want so much to know whether they've a fire in the winter: you never *can* tell, you know, unless our fire smokes, and then smoke comes up in that room too

– but that may be only pretence, just to make it look as if they had a fire. Well then, the books are something like our books, only the words go the wrong way; I know that, because I've held up one of our books to the glass, and then they hold up one in the other room.

'How would you like to live in Looking-glass House, Kitty? I wonder if they'd give you milk in there? Perhaps Looking-glass milk isn't good to drink. But oh, Kitty! now we come to the passage. You can just see a little *peep* of the passage in Looking-glass House, if you leave the door of our drawing-room wide open; and it's very like our passage as far as you can see, only you know it may be quite different on beyond. Oh, Kitty! how nice it would be if we could only get through into Looking-glass House! I'm sure it's got, oh! such beautiful things in it! Let's pretend there's a way of getting through into it somehow, Kitty. Let's pretend the glass has got all soft like gauze, so that we can get through. Why, it's turning into a sort of mist now, I declare! It'll be easy enough to get through—' She was up on the chimney-piece while she said this, though she hardly knew how she had got there. And certainly the glass *was* beginning to melt away, just like a bright silvery mist.

In another moment Alice was through the glass,

and had jumped lightly down into the Looking-glass room. The very first thing she did was to look whether there was a fire in the fireplace, and she was quite pleased to find that there was a real one, blazing away as brightly as the one she had left behind. 'So I shall be as warm here as I was in the old room,' thought Alice: 'warmer, in fact, because there'll be no one here to scold me away from the fire. Oh, what fun it'll be when they see me through the glass in here, and can't get at me!'

Then she began looking about, and noticed that what could be seen from the old room was quite common and uninteresting, but that all the rest was as different as possible. For instance, the pictures on the wall next to the fire seemed to be alive, and the very clock on the chimney-piece (you know you can only see the back of it in the Looking-glass) had got the face of a little old man and grinned at her.

GOBBOLINO THE WITCH'S CAT

by Ursula Moray Williams

When I was young I didn't own many books myself. I borrowed nearly all my books from the public library. If I close my eyes I can still picture that lovely room, full of children's books. Sometimes I looked for my favourite authors, sometimes I chose at random, but by the time I was eleven or twelve I'd read my way all round the room, from Louisa M. Alcott to Ursula Moray Williams.

Ursula Moray Williams wrote many books for children. I was especially fond of a book about a very large family called the Binklebys – it always made me laugh out loud. I also loved Gobbolino the Witch's Cat because it's such a touching, gentle book, and even the

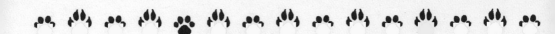

youngest reader can guess that things will work out for poor Gobbolino eventually.

I'd have liked a second book, about the adventures of Gobbolino's little sister Sootica. She's a far feistier character than her brother, desperate to start her apprenticeship as a witch's cat, and she mews for joy the first time she's taken for a ride on a broomstick.

JW

🐾 GOBBOLINO THE 🐾 WITCH'S CAT

One fine moonlit night little Gobbolino, the witch's kitten, and his sister Sootica tumbled out of the cavern where they had been born, to play at catch-a-mouse among the creeping shadows.

It was the first time they had left the cavern, and their round eyes were full of wonder and excitement at everything they saw.

Every leaf that blew, every dewdrop that glittered, every rustle in the forest around them set their furry black ears a-prick.

'Did you hear that, brother?'

'Did you see that, sister?'

'I saw it! *And that! And that! And that!*'

When they were tired of playing they sat side by side in the moonlight talking and quarrelling a little, as a witch's kittens will.

'What will you be when you grow up?' Gobbolino asked, as the moon began to sink behind the mountains and cocks crowed down the valley.

'Oh, I'll be a witch's cat like my ma,' said Sootica. 'I'll know all the Book of Magic off by heart and learn to ride a broomstick and turn mice into frogs and frogs into guinea-pigs. I'll fly down the clouds on the night-wind with the bats and the barn owls, saying, *"Meee-ee-ee-oww!"* so when people hear me coming they'll say: *"Hush! There goes Sootica, the witch's cat!"'*

Gobbolino was very silent when he heard his sister's fiery words.

'And what will you be, brother?' asked Sootica agreeably.

'I'll be a kitchen cat,' said Gobbolino. 'I'll sit by the fire with my paws tucked under my chest and sing like the kettle on the hob. When the children come in from school they'll pull my ears and tickle me under the chin and coax me round the kitchen with a cotton reel. I'll mind the house and keep down the mice and watch the baby, and when all the children are in bed I'll creep on my missus's lap while she darns the stockings and master nods in his chair. I'll stay with them for ever and ever, and they'll call me Gobbolino the kitchen cat.'

'Don't you want to be bad?' Sootica asked him in great surprise.

'No,' said Gobbolino, 'I want to be good and have people love me. People don't love witches' cats. They are too disagreeable.'

He licked his paw and began to wash his face, while his little sister scowled at him and was just about to trot in and find their mother, when a ray of moonlight falling across both the kittens set her fur standing on end with rage and fear.

'Brother! Brother! One of your paws is white!'

In the deeps of the witch's cavern no one had noticed that little Gobbolino had been born with a white front paw. Everyone knows this is quite wrong for witches' kittens, which are black all over from head to foot, but now the moonbeam lit up a pure white sock with five pink pads beneath it, while the kitten's coat, instead of being jet black like his sister's, had a faint sheen of tabby, and his lovely round eyes were blue! All witches' kittens are born with green eyes.

No wonder that little Sootica flew into the cavern

with cries of distress to tell her mother all about it.

'Ma! Ma! Our Gobbolino has a white sock! He has blue eyes! His coat is tabby, not black, and he wants to be a kitchen cat!'

The kitten's cries brought her mother Grimalkin to the door of the cavern. Their mistress, the witch, was not far behind her, and in less time than it takes to tell they had knocked the unhappy Gobbolino head over heels, set him on his feet again, cuffed his ears, tweaked his tail, bounced him, bullied him, and so bewildered him that he could only stare stupidly at them, blinking his beautiful blue eyes as if he could not imagine what they were so angry about.

At last Grimalkin picked him up by the scruff of his neck and dropped him in the darkest, dampest corner of the cavern among the witch's tame toads.

Gobbolino was afraid of the toads and shivered and shook all night.

THE CAT THAT WALKED BY HIMSELF

by Rudyard Kipling

My teacher used to read us Just So Stories *when I was at primary school. Maybe your teacher has read them to you, and even asked you to make up your own animal fable. The Cat That Walked by Himself has always been my favourite, though I dislike the passage where the wild Man throws his boots and little stone axe at the cat.*

The Cat in the story is such a real cat, so clever and artful. My Jacob is sometimes a cat who likes to walk by himself, waving his wild tail and walking by his wild lone – and he too will kill mice and be kind to babies just so long as they do not pull his tail too hard. Little Lily is unusually gregarious for a cat and will always choose to walk with Jacob rather than wander off by herself.

Thomas was the cat of mine who walked by himself – and went on walking. He was a little stray, a slinky black boy who slept under my garden shed and pressed his face longingly against the French windows, desperate to get indoors. He made friends with Jacob and did his best to ingratiate himself with me, lying down and waving his paws, trying to make himself look as cute as possible.

It worked. Thomas lived with me very happily for two years. Then he started getting into violent scraps with a new fierce cat living further up the road. He began to stay out longer and longer, and didn't seem very hungry when he came home. He was clearly being fed somewhere else. Then one day he sauntered off – and never came back.

I went up and down the roads searching for him, I leafleted the neighbourhood with his photo, and stuck posters on lampposts. I phoned all the nearby vets, because Thomas had been chipped and so could easily be traced. No one had seen hide nor hair of him.

He might have been in some terrible accident, of course – but I like to think he'd simply decided it was time to stroll off elsewhere. I hope he's very happy, wherever he is now. My heart still stops whenever I

see a sleek little black cat running along the pavement. It's never Thomas – but I still haven't given up
hope that he'll stop walking by his wild lone and come
back home.

J~S

🐾 THE CAT THAT 🐾 WALKED BY HIMSELF

Hear and attend and listen; for this befell and be-happened and became and was, O my Best Beloved, when the Tame animals were wild. The Dog was wild, and the Horse was wild, and the Cow was wild, and the Sheep was wild, and the Pig was wild – as wild as wild could be – and they walked in the Wet Wild Woods by their wild lones. But the wildest of all the wild animals was the Cat. He walked by himself, and all places were alike to him.

Of course the Man was wild too. He was dreadfully wild. He didn't even begin to be tame till he met the

Woman, and she told him that she did not like living in his wild ways. She picked out a nice dry Cave, instead of a heap of wet leaves, to lie down in; and she strewed clean sand on the floor; and she lit a nice fire of wood at the back of the Cave; and she hung a dried wild-horse skin, tail-down, across the opening of the Cave; and she said, 'Wipe your feet, dear, when you come in, and now we'll keep house.'

That night, Best Beloved, they ate wild sheep roasted on the hot stones, and flavoured with wild garlic and wild pepper; and wild duck stuffed with wild rice and wild fenugreek and wild coriander; and marrow-bones of wild oxen; and wild cherries, and wild grenadillas. Then the Man went to sleep in front of the fire ever so happy; but the Woman sat up, combing her hair. She took the bone of the shoulder of mutton – the big flat blade-bone – and she looked at the wonderful marks on it, and she threw more wood on the fire, and she made a Magic. She made the First Singing Magic in the world.

Out in the Wet Wild Woods all the wild animals gathered together where they could see the light of the fire a long way off, and they wondered what it meant.

Then Wild Horse stamped with his wild foot and said, 'O my Friends and O my Enemies, why have the

Man and the Woman made that great light in that great Cave, and what harm will it do us?'

Wild Dog lifted up his wild nose and smelled the smell of the roast mutton, and said, 'I will go up and see and look, and say; for I think it is good. Cat, come with me.'

'Nenni!' said the Cat. 'I am the Cat who walks by himself, and all places are alike to me. I will not come.'

'Then we can never be friends again,' said Wild Dog, and he trotted off to the Cave. But when he had gone a little way the Cat said to himself, 'All places are alike to me. Why should I not go too and see and look and come away at my own liking?' So he slipped after Wild Dog softly, very softly, and hid himself where he could hear everything.

When Wild Dog reached the mouth of the Cave he lifted up the dried horse-skin with his nose and sniffed the beautiful smell of the roast mutton, and the Woman, looking at the blade-bone, heard him, and laughed, and said, 'Here comes the first. Wild Thing out of the Wild Woods, what do you want?'

Wild Dog said, 'O my Enemy and Wife of my Enemy, what is this that smells so good in the Wild Woods?'

Then the Woman picked up a roasted mutton-bone and threw it to the Wild Dog, and said, 'Wild

Thing out of the Wild Woods, taste and try.' Wild Dog gnawed the bone, and it was more delicious than anything he had ever tasted, and he said, 'O my Enemy and Wife of my Enemy, give me another.'

The Woman said, 'Wild Thing out of the Wild Woods, help my Man to hunt through the day and guard this Cave at night, and I will give you as many roast bones as you need.'

'Ah!' said the Cat, listening. 'This is a very wise Woman, but she is not so wise as I am.'

Wild Dog crawled into the Cave and laid his head on the Woman's lap, and said, 'O my Friend and Wife of my Friend, I will help your Man to hunt through the day, and at night I will guard your Cave.'

'Ah!' said the Cat, listening. 'That is a very foolish Dog.' And he went back through the Wet Wild Woods waving his wild tail, and walking by his wild lone. But he never told anybody.

When the Man waked up he said, 'What is Wild Dog doing here?' And the Woman said, 'His name is not Wild Dog any more, but the First Friend, because he will be our friend for always and always and always. Take him with you when you go hunting.'

Next night the Woman cut great green armfuls of fresh grass from the water-meadows, and dried it before the fire, so that it smelt like new-mown hay, and she sat at the mouth of the Cave and plaited a halter out of horse-hide, and she looked at the shoulder-of-mutton bone – at the big broad blade-bone – and she made a Magic. She made the Second Singing Magic in the world.

Out in the Wild Woods all the wild animals wondered what had happened to the Wild Dog, and at last Wild Horse stamped his foot and said, 'I will go and see and say why Wild Dog has not returned. Cat, come with me.'

'Nenni!' said the Cat. 'I am the Cat who walks by himself, and all places are alike to me. I will not come.' But all the same he followed Wild Horse softly, very softly, and hid himself where he could hear everything.

When the Woman heard Wild Horse tripping and stumbling on his long mane, she laughed and said, 'Here comes the second. Wild Thing out of the Wild Woods, what do you want?'

Wild Horse said, 'O my Enemy and Wife of my Enemy, where is Wild Dog?'

The woman laughed, and picked up the blade-bone and looked at it, and said, 'Wild Thing out of the Wild Woods, you did not come here for Wild Dog, but for the sake of this good grass.'

And Wild Horse, tripping and stumbling on his

long mane, said, 'That is true; give it me to eat.'

The Woman said, 'Wild Thing out of the Wild Woods, bend your wild head and wear what I give you, and you shall eat the wonderful grass three times a day.'

'Ah,' said the Cat, listening, 'this is a clever Woman, but she is not so clever as I am.'

Wild Horse bent his wild head, and the Woman slipped the plaited hide halter over it, and Wild Horse breathed on the Woman's feet and said, 'O my Mistress, and Wife of my Master, I will be your servant for the sake of the wonderful grass.'

'Ah,' said the Cat, listening, 'that is a very foolish Horse.' And he went back through the Wet Wild Woods, waving his wild tail and walking by his wild lone. But he never told anybody.

When the Man and the Dog came back from hunting, the Man said, 'What is Wild Horse doing here?' And the Woman said, 'His name is not Wild Horse any more, but the first Servant, because he will carry us from place to place for always and always and always. Ride on his back when you go hunting.'

Next day, holding her wild head high that her wild horns should not catch in the wild trees, Wild Cow came up to the Cave, and the Cat followed, and hid himself just the same as before; and everything happened just the same as before; and the Cat said the same things as before; and when Wild Cow had promised to give her milk to the Woman every day in exchange for the wonderful grass, the Cat went back through the Wet Wild Woods waving his wild tail and walking by his wild lone, just the same as before. But he never told anybody. And when the Man and the Horse and the Dog came home from hunting and asked the same questions same as before, the Woman said, 'Her name is not Wild Cow any more, but the Giver of Good Food. She will give us the warm white milk for always and always and always, and I will take care of her while you and the First Friend and the First Servant go hunting.'

Next day the Cat waited to see if any other Wild Thing would go up to the Cave, but no one moved in the Wet Wild Woods, so the Cat walked there by himself; and he saw the Woman milking the Cow, and he saw the light of the fire in the Cave, and he smelt the smell of the warm white milk.

Cat said, 'O my Enemy and Wife of my Enemy, where did Wild Cow go?'

The Woman laughed and said, 'Wild Thing out of the Wild Woods, go back to the Woods again, for I have braided up my hair, and I have put away the magic blade-bone, and we have no more need of either friends or servants in our Cave.'

Cat said, 'I am not a friend, and I am not a servant. I am the Cat who walks by himself, and I wish to come into your Cave.'

Woman said, 'Then why did you not come with First Friend on the first night?'

Cat grew very angry and said, 'Has Wild Dog told tales of me?'

Then the Woman laughed and said, 'You are the Cat who walks by himself, and all places are alike to you. You are neither a friend nor a servant. You have said it yourself. Go away and walk by yourself in all places alike.'

Then Cat pretended to be sorry and said, 'Must I never come into the Cave? Must I never sit by the warm fire? Must I never drink the warm white milk? You are very wise and very beautiful. You should not be cruel even to a Cat.'

Woman said, 'I knew I was wise, but I did not know I was beautiful. So I will make a bargain with you. If ever I say one word in your praise, you may come into the Cave.'

'And if you say two words in my praise?' said the Cat.

'I never shall,' said the Woman, 'but if I say two words in your praise, you may sit by the fire in the cave.'

'And if you say three words?' said the Cat.

'I never shall,' said the Woman, 'but if I say three words in your praise, you may drink the warm white milk three times a day for always and always and always.'

Then the Cat arched his back and said, 'Now let the Curtain at the mouth of the Cave, and the Fire at the back of the Cave, and the Milk-pots that stand beside the Fire, remember what my Enemy and the Wife of my Enemy has said.' And he went away through the Wet Wild Woods waving his wild tail and walking by his wild lone.

That night when the Man and the Horse and the Dog came home from hunting, the Woman did not tell them of the bargain that she had made with the Cat, because she was afraid that they might not like it.

Cat went far and far away and hid himself in the Wet Wild Woods by his wild lone for a long time till the Woman forgot all about him. Only the Bat – the little upside-down Bat – that hung inside the Cave knew where Cat hid; and every evening Bat would fly to Cat with news of what was happening.

One evening Bat said, 'There is a Baby in the Cave. He is new and pink and fat and small, and the Woman is very fond of him.'

'Ah,' said the Cat, listening, 'but what is the Baby fond of?'

'He is fond of things that are soft and tickle,' said the Bat. 'He is fond of warm things to hold in his arms when he goes to sleep. He is fond of being played with. He is fond of all those things.'

'Ah,' said the Cat, listening, 'then my time has come.'

Next night Cat walked through the Wet Wild Woods and hid very near the Cave till morning-time, and Man and Dog and Horse went hunting. The Woman was busy cooking that morning, and the Baby cried and interrupted. So she carried him outside the Cave and gave him a handful of pebbles to play with. But still the Baby cried.

Then the Cat put out his paddy paw and patted the Baby on the cheek, and it cooed; and the Cat rubbed against its fat knees and tickled it under its fat chin with his tail. And the Baby laughed; and the Woman heard him and smiled.

Then the Bat – the little upside-down Bat – that hung in the mouth of the Cave said, 'O my Hostess and Wife of my Host and Mother of my Host's Son, a Wild Thing from the Wild Woods is most beautifully playing with your Baby.'

'A blessing on that Wild Thing whoever he may be,' said the Woman, straightening her back, 'for I was a busy woman this morning and he has done me a service.'

That very minute and second, Best Beloved, the dried horse-skin Curtain that was stretched tail-down at the mouth of the Cave fell down – *woosh!* – because it remembered the bargain she had made with the Cat; and when the Woman went to pick it up – lo and behold! – the Cat was sitting quite comfy inside the Cave.

'O my Enemy and Wife of my Enemy and Mother of my Enemy,' said the Cat, 'it is I: for you have spoken a word in my praise, and now I can sit within the Cave for always and always and always. But still I am the cat who walks by himself, and all places are alike to me.'

The Woman was very angry, and shut her lips tight and took up her spinning-wheel and began to spin.

But the Baby cried because the Cat had gone away, and the Woman could not hush it, for it struggled and kicked and grew black in the face.

'O my Enemy and Wife of my Enemy and Mother of my Enemy,' said the Cat, 'take a strand of the thread that you are spinning and tie it to your spinning-whorl and drag it along the floor, and I will show you a Magic that shall make your Baby laugh as loudly as he is now crying.'

'I will do so,' said the Woman, 'because I am at my wits' end; but I will not thank you for it.'

She tied the thread to the little clay spindle-whorl and drew it across the floor, and the Cat ran after it and patted it with his paws and rolled head over heels, and tossed it backward over his shoulder and chased it between his hind-legs and pretended to lose it, and pounced down upon it again, till the Baby laughed as loudly as it had been crying, and scrambled after the Cat and frolicked all over the Cave till it grew tired and settled down to sleep with the Cat in its arms.

'Now,' said Cat, 'I will sing the Baby a song that shall keep him asleep for an hour.' And he began to purr, loud and low, low and loud, till the Baby fell fast asleep. The Woman smiled as she looked down upon the two of them, and said, 'That was wonderfully done. No question but you are very clever, O Cat.'

That very minute and second, Best Beloved, the smoke of the Fire at the back of the Cave came down in clouds from the roof – *puff!* – because it remembered the bargain she had made with the Cat; and when it had cleared away – lo and behold! – the Cat was sitting quite comfy close to the fire.

'O my Enemy and Wife of my Enemy and Mother of my Enemy,' said the Cat, 'it is I: for you have spoken a second word in my praise, and now I can sit by the warm fire at the back of the Cave for always and always and always. But still I am the Cat who walks by himself, and all places are alike to me.'

Then the Woman was very very angry, and let down her hair and put more wood on the fire and brought out the broad blade-bone of the shoulder of mutton and began to make a Magic that should prevent her from saying a third word in praise of the Cat. It was not a Singing Magic, Best Beloved, it was a Still Magic; and by and by the Cave grew so still that a little wee-wee mouse crept out of a corner and ran across the floor.

'O my Enemy and Wife of my Enemy and Mother of my Enemy,' said the Cat, 'is that little mouse part of your Magic?'

'Ouh! Chee! No indeed!' said the Woman, and she dropped the blade-bone and jumped upon the footstool in front of the fire and braided up her hair very quick for fear that the mouse should run up it.

'Ah,' said the Cat, watching, 'then the mouse will do me no harm if I eat it?'

'No,' said the Woman, braiding up her hair, 'eat it quickly and I will ever be grateful to you.'

Cat made one jump and caught the little mouse, and the Woman said, 'A hundred thanks. Even the First Friend is not quick enough to catch little mice as you have done. You must be very wise.'

That very moment and second, O Best Beloved, the Milk-pot that stood by the fire cracked in two pieces – *ffft!* – because it remembered the bargain she had made with the Cat; and when the Woman jumped down from the footstool – lo and behold! – the Cat was lapping up the warm white milk that lay in one of the broken pieces.

'O my Enemy and Wife of my Enemy and Mother of my Enemy,' said the Cat, 'it is I: for you have spoken three words in my praise, and now I can drink the warm white milk three times a day for always and always and always. But *still* I am the Cat who walks by himself, and all places are alike to me.'

Then the Woman laughed and set the Cat a bowl of the warm white milk and said, 'O Cat, you are as clever as a Man, but remember that your bargain was not made with the Man or the Dog, and I do not know what they will do when they come home.'

'What is that to me?' said the Cat. 'If I have my place in the Cave by the fire and my warm white milk three times a day I do not care what the Man or the Dog can do.'

That evening when the Man and the Dog came into the Cave, the Woman told them all the story of the bargain, while the Cat sat by the fire and smiled. Then the Man said, 'Yes, but he has not made a bargain, with *me* or with all proper Men after me.' Then he took off his two leather boots and he took up his little stone axe (that makes three) and he fetched a piece of wood and a hatchet (that is five altogether), and he set them out in a row and he said, 'Now we will make *our* bargain. If you do not catch mice when you are in the Cave for always and always and always, I will throw these five things at you whenever I see you, and so shall all proper Men do after me.'

'Ah,' said the Woman, listening, 'this is a very clever Cat, but he is not so clever as my Man.'

The Cat counted the five things (and they looked very knobby) and he said, 'I will catch mice when I am in the Cave for always and always and always; but *still* I am the Cat who walks by himself, and all places are alike to me.'

'Not when I am near,' said the Man. 'If you had not said that last I would have put all these things away for always and always and always; but now I am going to throw my two boots and my little stone axe (that makes three) at you whenever I meet you. And so shall all proper Men do after me!'

Then the Dog said, 'Wait a minute. He has not made a bargain with *me* or with all proper Dogs after me.' And he showed his teeth and said, 'If you are not kind to the Baby while I am in the Cave for always and always and always, I will hunt you till I catch you, and when I catch you I will bite you. And so shall all proper Dogs do after me.'

'Ah,' said the Woman, listening, 'this is a very clever Cat, but he is not so clever as the Dog.'

Cat counted the Dog's teeth (and they looked very pointed) and he said, 'I will be kind to the Baby while I am in the Cave, as long as he does not pull my tail too hard, for always and always and always. But *still* I am the Cat that walks by himself, and all places are alike to me!'

'Not when I am near,' said the Dog. 'If you had not said that last I would have shut my mouth for always and always and always; but *now* I am going to hunt you up a tree whenever I meet you. And so shall all proper Dogs do after me.'

Then the man threw his two boots and his little stone axe (that makes three) at the Cat, and the Cat ran out of the Cave and the Dog chased him up a tree; and from that day to this, Best Beloved, three proper Men out of five will always throw things at a Cat whenever they meet him, and all proper Dogs will chase him up a tree. But the Cat keeps his side of the bargain too. He will kill mice, and he will be kind to Babies when he is in the house, just as long as they do not pull his tail too hard. But when he has done that, and between times, and when the moon gets up and night comes, he is the Cat that walks by himself, and all places are alike to him. Then he goes out to the Wet Wild Woods or up the Wet Wild Trees or on the Wet Wild Roofs, waving his wild tail and walking by his wild lone.

ORLANDO'S INVISIBLE PYJAMAS

by Kathleen Hale

Do you or any of your friends have a ginger tom cat? He might very well be called Orlando, after the most famous cat in children's literature, Orlando the Marmalade Cat. They are gorgeous, sophisticated books that you can devour when you're long past the picture-book stage. I love them all, but I have an especial spot for Orlando's Invisible Pyjamas. *It's such a tender book. I adore the passage where Orlando's wife Grace says she will knit him a pair of pyjama trousers that will match his fur exactly because 'I know your stripes by heart.'*

Until I reread the book today I'd completely forgotten that Orlando's former girlfriend was a glamorous cat

called Queenie. In my book *Queenie, that fluffy white Queenie cat has a litter of four kittens at the end of the story. One is ginger, and two are ginger and white, so it's clear she has a ginger admirer. I wonder if it was Orlando . . .*

Jₙₛ

🐾 ORLANDO'S INVISIBLE 🐾 PYJAMAS

Orlando breathed a hole in the frost pattern on the window and watched the thick snow falling softly. It was evening; the three kittens were in bed and his dear wife Grace was knitting cat-traps to protect the robins she loved so much.

'They are such sweet little birds I feel I could eat them,' she said, 'but if I hang these nets round the tree trunks, we can't climb up to catch them.'

A faint glow of light shone through the swirling snowflakes; it shone from the night-watchman's lantern on the road.

'He must be lonely sitting out there all night, guarding that big hole the roadmenders are making bigger,' thought Orlando. 'I'll go and have a chat with him and take him a mouse for his supper.'

He took one from the larder and crept past the sleeping kittens. Tinkle, the black one, opened one eye and said, 'Hello, Farver, you've grown a Moustache!'

Orlando winked at him and set out on his journey through the snow. To a cat, snow-flakes seemed as large as snowballs; sometimes Orlando disappeared into a drift that would only have reached a little girl's knee.

Orlando plodded on till he found Mr Pusey, the night-watchman; the old man was frying his supper.

'Good evening,' said Orlando.

'Oo,' replied Mr Pusey, 'Oi be glad to zee you this murksome night! Oi thought as all folks in the world had been bewitched into snow-flakes – not a soul to be seen, and Oi wondering when the spell would be cast on me.'

'Well,' said Orlando, 'here's a fine mouse for your supper.' He jumped on to a paraffin can the better to pop it into Mr Pusey's frying pan.

'Oo! Oi wouldn't deprive ye!' the old man said hastily. 'You have it, me boy!' He picked the mouse out of the pan quickly. The can tipped over and Orlando fell off; his hind legs and tail were drenched with paraffin.

It smelt nasty and burnt him. He plunged into the cold snow and rolled, but that did no good. He dashed home to Grace.

Grace tried so hard with the kittens' help to wash her dear husband clean, but the paraffin nearly suffocated her and burnt her poor tongue terribly.

At dawn, after a restless night, Orlando crept out of the house feeling uncomfortable and miserable.

All day Grace waited for him to return. By tea time she was frantic.

'Oh my beloved husband!' she cried. 'What has happened to you?'

The kittens helped her to search the house and then the garden. Snow had covered Orlando's footprints and it was bitterly cold. The kittens wore their muffs.

Not a bird dared open its beak for fear of a frozen tongue.

Blanche, the white kitten, set out across the white lawn; Pansy, the tortoiseshell one, climbed up the black and white trees for a better view, while Tinkle pushed his way into the pampas grass. Grace called loudly for Orlando, her voice rang out clearly in the silence.

Suddenly Tinkle found the tip of a pink snake. Very cautiously he patted it. It twitched but did him no harm; he sniffed along it until he came to – Orlando sitting on the other end! The snake was Orlando's tail!

Poor Orlando, he was quite bald from his waist to the tip of his tail; the paraffin had taken off all his fur.

He hissed at Tinkle and crept further into the frosty bushes. Tinkle was frightened and called his mother.

Orlando told them he was sorry for being cross with Tinkle, but they must leave him, for he could not bear to be seen like this.

'We'll never leave you!' said Grace firmly. 'Don't stare at your father,' she told the kittens who had gathered round. 'He is unhappy. We must think of a way to get him home without being seen by the neighbours.'

'Let's make him a Modesty Awning to hide him on his way back,' suggested Pansy.

Pansy told them how to make one. The kittens collected moss, dead leaves and twigs which Grace stitched on to a white towel. It looked just like the snowy landscape; they draped it over Grace's ironing board and carried it on their heads to where Orlando lay shivering.

'We'll hold this over you while you walk home,' Grace explained to him, 'and nobody will see you.'

The strange little procession reached home unseen, and Grace put Orlando to bed with a Hot Wartle (Tinkle's name for a hot water bottle). She gave him a bowl of warm haddock milk.

'I'll knit you a pair of pyjama trousers so like your own fur that nobody will see the difference,' said Grace. 'I know your stripes by heart.'

Mr Pusey came to enquire after Orlando, who showed him the damage done by the paraffin. Mr Pusey was very upset and pursed up his mouth like a spout; he promised not to tell the neighbours how queer Orlando looked. Every day he came and played Snakes and Ladders with Orlando, to help him to pass the time till the pyjamas were ready.

The kittens loved Mr Pusey. Blanche and Pansy felt sorry for the old man who lived out of doors in all weathers. They washed his hands for him, and tidied his eyebrows.

'Daughters are surely a great blessing, Madam,' he said to Grace.

Tinkle rummaged among the bits of cheese and toffee papers in Mr Pusey's pocket. He purred loudly and sang:

'I love little Pusey
His coat is so warm.'

Towards evening Mr Pusey had to go back to his work. Lanterns must be lit and placed round the hole in the road to prevent people from falling into it in the dark.

Orlando grew weary with lying in bed and was terribly afraid that he would be bald for life.

Grace was too busy knitting the pyjamas to entertain him, but the kittens did their best.

'We're going to tell you our dreams, every day,' Tinkle told him. 'Blanche'll begin, then Pansy next. Mine's much the best one so you'd better hear it last.'

'I dramp,' began Blanche, 'that I had a dear little balloon which floated me up to Birds' Heaven. I was given a drink of magic milk which stopped me wanting to eat the bird-angels. They taught me how to fly, and I had Angel cake for elevenses. One day a darling little girl egg was laid, and I was afraid she'd fall to earth and be smashed. But she grew wings just in time, and then I woke up. D'you like my dream?' she asked Orlando anxiously. Orlando did, very much.

Pansy continued: 'I dreempt I was two kittens,

a black one at night and a ginger one by day. Each of me had nine lives, so I had eighteen altogether. I got twice as much to eat because they thought I was two kittens. But I got in a muddle and the black one came out in the daytime, and they said, "We fed her last night so she doesn't want another meal now." So I decided to wake up.'

'Now it's MY turn!' said Tinkle. 'I drump I had a lorry-load of ice-cream – that's all, and can I have a shilling please?' he asked Orlando.

'You can have tuppence,' said Orlando, smiling.

'Huh. *That's* not much to help me on my grown-up way,' grumbled Tinkle.

The dreams were soon told and Orlando began to worry about himself again.

Tinkle was sorry for him, and ashamed of grumbling: he wanted to please Orlando more than ever.

'Tell us a story of your yoof,' he suggested, for he knew that people liked nothing better than to talk about themselves.

'A story of my youth?' replied Orlando. 'Well, if you bring me the family photograph album, the pictures will remind me of things.'

Orlando turned to the first page, and the kittens gathered round.

'Here is my Great-Great-Great-Great-Great-Aunt

Caterina in the bicycling bloomers that were the fashion in those days. And here is Great-Great-Great-Great-Great-Uncle Tom with his hounds and his hunter, in front of his country mansion . . . Aha!' laughed Orlando, already cheering up. 'Here I am as a baby lying on a fur rug.

'This is my school football team with me in the centre. Here I am with the prize I won for my essay called "Man, the Animal".'

Orlando passed over the next page, but Pansy made him turn back to it. 'Whose picture is that?' she asked.

'That?' answered Orlando vaguely. 'Oh, just a girl called Queenie.'

'Let me see too!' cried Grace. 'Oh, what lovely whiskers she has, and what a beautiful hat . . .'

Grace felt sad, and ashamed of her homely apron.

'Fine clothes and false whiskers don't always make good wives,' said Orlando. 'Your speckled whiskers are very pretty, darling, and nobody dresses as wonderfully as you.

'Now, kittens, here's your Mother, when I first met her. It was during winter sports and she was trying to teach herself to ski. Naturally I helped her, and we've helped each other ever since in every kind of way.

'I was a naughty kitten sometimes,' Orlando

continued, closing the album. 'Once I rubbed some mustard on my nose to make it red and look as though I had a cold. Mother kept me at home from school for two lovely days, which was just what I wanted.

'One day Mother gave a tea party for all her lady friends. They were so stiff and polite that I locked them in the drawing room, and they had to climb out through the window. I laughed so much that I felt quite good for a long time after.'

Orlando fell asleep, happier than he had been for a long time.

'That *was* a good idea of yours, Tinkle,' whispered Grace.

By the time Orlando woke up, the moon had risen and the pyjamas were finished; Blanche and Pansy had fluffed up the wool to make it look like real fur.

'Now Queenie would never have made these!' exclaimed Orlando delightedly. 'Only you, dear Grace. I'll put them on and we'll all go for a walk.'

The pyjamas fitted him perfectly; it was impossible to see where they began, and he ended.

The cats visited Mr Pusey, who thought Orlando's fur had grown again.

'Oo, how glad Oi be to zee you!' he said. 'Have a sausage to wipe out all sad remembrances, and a drink of tea to wash away cruel happenings!'

Orlando explained the pyjamas to him, but Mr Pusey insisted that they should eat a sausage, 'to bolster up hope,' he said, 'and drink some tea, for as rain causes grass to grow, maybe it'll make fur sprout.'

On the way home they met a dog. All their fur stood on end except where Orlando wore his pyjamas. The dog laughed at this and made rude remarks. The cats hurried by in confusion.

The time came when Grace wanted to wash the pyjamas. Sadly Orlando went back to bed and took them off. To his surprise, instead of finding his naked flesh, there appeared to be another pair of pyjamas covering him.

'How clever of you, Grace, to have made a lining . . . I needn't stay in bed after all!'

'A lining?' replied Grace, puzzled. 'That's no lining,' she cried with delight, 'that's your own fur which has grown at last!'

The cats were too happy to speak; they purred loudly until they sneezed.

Orlando decided to present the pyjamas to the Anti-Fur-Trappers' League for their museum to show people how lovely imitation fur can be.

The Presentation of the Invisible Pyjamas took place in the Town Hall, and the building was crowded. There were long and eloquent speeches, during which

Orlando and Grace sat modestly in the limelight.

On the way home the cats met the rude dog again, but when he saw the whole of Orlando's fur rise on end, he ran off quickly on a pretend errand.

'All's well, when ends are well,' said Tinkle with a grin.

SOFFRONA AND HER CAT MUFF

by Mary Martha Sherwood

This is a very old-fashioned story because it was written nearly two hundred years ago. At first glance it seems a little quaint, especially when the author starts quoting passages from the Bible. Mrs Sherwood is like a very strict teacher, keen to give a moral message and tell children how to behave. You might find this a bit off-putting, but she's actually a very good story-teller too. Soffrona is a very real little girl – she's desperate to make the rescued kitten her special cat and she gets irritated with Jane, the servant, who says in exasperation, 'You can think of nothing but cats.' If you can think of nothing but cats, then I think you'll like this story.

JwS

❧ SOFFRONA AND ❧ HER CAT MUFF

Little Soffrona lived with a lady who loved her very much. She was not the lady's own child, but she was as dear to that lady as if she had been so, and the child always called her mamma. The lady had a little girl of her own called Sophia. Sophia was one year older than Soffrona; and Sophia and Soffrona learned lessons together, and played together, and were very happy in each other's company. When you saw Soffrona, you might be sure Sophia was not very far off; and when you saw Sophia, it was very certain that Soffrona was at no great distance.

How delightful it is for little children to live in love and peace one with another! Hear what David says on this subject – *Behold, how good and pleasant it is for brethren to dwell together in unity!* (Psalm. 133:1)

Soffrona and Sophia lived in a very lovely house, surrounded with woods. Wherever you looked from the windows of that house, you might see trees growing thickly together, forming beautiful arbours, and pleasant shades, with little paths winding about among those trees; and here and there, near the trees, were fountains of water springing from the hills, and running down into the valleys: for there were hills there, and the tops of some of them were covered all through the winter with snow, though in summer they appeared green or blue, according to the time of the year, and wore a very pleasant aspect.

Soffrona and Sophia were allowed to play in these woods, and they had learned to run and skip upon the hills like young fawns. It was very pleasing to see them, and they found many treasures in those wild places which children who have never been in woods have no idea of. They found snail-shells, and painting-stones, and wild strawberries, and bil-berries, and walnuts, and hazel nuts, and beautiful moss, and many kinds of flowers; and there they heard birds sing – cuckoos, and linnets, and blackbirds, and thrushes; and saw beautiful butterflies with gold and purple plumes, and dragon-flies, whose wings look like fine silk net.

One morning in the month of May, Soffrona and Sophia had leave given to them to play in the woods, after they had finished their lessons, and they took a basket with them, to bring home any treasures which they might find. And they went a long way through the woods – I dare say as much as half a mile – till they came to a place where an old tree had been blown down by the side of a brook; and there they sat down, and each of them took a little penny book to read out of their basket: and while they were reading, they heard a noise of boys shouting and laughing, and they jumped up and hid themselves behind some bushes.

So the boys came nearer, and went down close to the water's side; and the little girls heard them say to one another, 'Let us put it in the deepest place, where it cannot scramble out.' And they saw the boys stoop over the water and put something into it, and at the same time they heard a very young kitten cry; and the two little girls could not stop themselves from screaming out, quite loud, from the midst of the bushes, saying, 'Wicked, cruel boys! what are you doing?'

Now the boys heard the cries of the little girls;

and, as the Bible says, *The wicked flee when no man pursueth;* (Prov. 28:1) so they all took to their heels, and ran away as fast as they could, leaving the poor little kitten in the water.

Soffrona and Sophia did not lose one moment after the boys were gone, but ran to the brook, and found the little kitten almost dead. However, they got it out, though they wet themselves up to the knees in so doing, and they returned to the tree, and Soffrona sat down, and laid it upon her lap, while Sophia wiped it dry; and as she rubbed it, she found warmth returning to its little body, and presently it opened its eyes and began to mew. 'O my dear little Puss!' said Soffrona, 'how very glad I am that you are not dead! You shall be my Puss, and I will call you Muff. Will you let her be mine, Sophia? Will you give me your share of her?'

Sophia did not say a word against this request, for it was the same to her whether the little kitten was called hers or Soffrona's, and she liked to oblige Soffrona: besides, Sophia was a year older than Soffrona, and it might be expected that she would be more moderate in her desires, and think less of herself. Sophia had lived twelve months longer than Soffrona in the world; and how much may a person learn, with the blessing of God, in twelve months!

So it was agreed that the kitten should belong to Soffrona, and be called Muff; and when the little girls had dried it as well as they could they put it into the basket upon some soft moss, and ran home with it.

The lady was not angry with them for having wetted themselves in the brook to save a poor little animal's life, but she hastened to change their clothes; and then they took the kitten out of the basket, and procured some milk to feed it with.

When the fur of the little cat was quite dry, it was seen that she was very beautifully marked. Her legs, and face, and breast, were quite white, and her back was streaked with yellow and black; so that she appeared like a fine polished tortoiseshell. But she was only nine or ten days old, and was not able to lap milk; and this was a great grief to Soffrona and Sophia, for they feared that although she had been saved from the water, she would surely die of hunger. The little girls tried to force milk down her throat with a spoon, but the milk ran down the outside of her mouth, instead of the inside of her throat, and the little creature's sides became quite hollow for want of nourishment.

Soffrona was thinking of nothing but Muff all the evening, and she kept her on her lap while she was reading and while she was eating her supper. She was, indeed, so much occupied by her little kitten, that, when the lady asked her to help to make a flannel petticoat for a poor old woman who lived in a cottage among the hills, not very far off, she took the needle in her hand, it is true, but I do not think that she took twenty stitches; for she was looking down every minute upon the kitten on her lap: and the petticoat would not have been done that night, if Sophia had not been doubly diligent.

Now it was much to be wished that the petticoat should be done that night; for it was intended for a good old woman who lived in the woods, a very poor woman indeed, and the March winds had given her great pain in her limbs, and she was in much need of a warm petticoat; and more than that, the lady had promised the little girls the pleasure of taking the petticoat, with some tea and sugar the next morning, after they had repeated their lessons, to the cottage. But, as I before said, Soffrona's heart was with her kitten, and she could think of nothing else, and of no other creature. She had no pity left for the old woman, so much was she thinking of little Muff. We ought to be kind to animals; but our first affections should be given to our Maker, our second to our fellow-creatures, and our third to any poor animals which may be in our power.

The last thing Soffrona did in the evening, was to try to put some milk down Muff's throat, and this was the first thing she did in the morning, and so far she did right, for the poor little thing depended on her. But when she had done all she could for Muff, she should have given her mind to her other duties; but she could not command herself to attend to any thing else all that morning, and learned her lessons so ill, that, if the lady had not been very indulgent, she would have deprived her of the pleasure of walking with Sophia to see the old woman, and to carry the petticoat.

There was a neat little maid-servant, called Jane, who used to walk out with Sophia and Soffrona when they had a long way to go; and Jane was ready waiting for the little girls by the time the lessons were done.

Sophia had asked leave to carry the basket with the petticoat and the tea and sugar: and Soffrona took another basket, and put a bit of flannel at the bottom of it, and laid Muff in it, and tied the cover over it; and when Sophia took up her basket to carry, Soffrona also put her arm under the handle of Muff's basket, and went downstairs with it.

When they were got out of the house, Jane said, 'What, have you two baskets, young ladies, full of good things, to carry to old Martha? Well, I am very glad; for she is a good and pious old woman.'

Soffrona coloured, but did not answer, and Sophia smiled, and said, 'She has not got any thing for the old woman in her basket: she has only got Muff, wrapped in flannel, in it.'

'O, Miss!' said Jane, 'how can you think of doing such a thing? What a trouble it will be to you to carry the kitten all the way! And we have two miles to walk, and most of it uphill. Please to let me carry the kitten back to the house.'

'No, no, Jane,' said Soffrona, 'no, you shall not.'

'*Shall* not, Miss!' said Jane: 'is that a pretty word?'

Soffrona looked very cross, and Jane was turning back to complain to the lady: but Sophia entreated her not to do it; and Soffrona submitted to ask her pardon for being rude, and promised to behave better, if she would permit her to carry the kitten where she was going. So that matter was settled, and Jane and the little girls proceeded.

I could tell you much about the pretty places through which they passed in going to poor Martha's cottage, which were quite new to the little girls. They first went through some dark woods, where the trees met over their heads like the arches in a church; and then they came to a dingle, where water was running at the bottom, and they crossed the water by a wooden bridge; then they had to climb up such a steep, such a very steep hill, covered with bushes; then they came to a high field surrounded with trees, and in a corner of that field was old Martha's thatched cottage. It was a poor place: the walls were black-and-white, and there were two windows, one of which was in the thatch, and one below, and a door, half of which was open; for it was such a door as you see in cottages, the lower part of which can be shut while the other is open. There was a little smoke coming out of the chimney, for Martha was cooking her potatoes for her dinner.

'Do you think Martha has any milk in her house?' said Soffrona; 'for poor Muff must be very hungry by this time.'

'I fear not,' replied Jane: 'but come, young ladies, we have been a long time getting up this hill, and we must be at home by three o'clock.'

So they went on, and came close to the door, and stood there a little while, looking in. They saw within the cottage a very small kitchen; but it was neat, and there was nothing out of its place. There was a wide chimney in the kitchen, and in the chimney a fire of sticks, over which hung a little kettle. Old Martha was sitting on a stool within the chimney. She was dressed in a blue petticoat and jacket, and had a high crowned, old-fashioned felt hat on her head, and a coarse clean check handkerchief on her neck. Before her was a spinning-wheel, which she was turning very diligently, for she could not see to do any work besides spinning; and by the fire, on the hob, sat a fine tortoise-shell cat, which was the old woman's only companion. 'O!' cried little Soffrona, 'there is a cat! I see a cat!'

'Dear, Miss,' said Jane, 'you can think of nothing but cats.'

'Well, Jane,' answered Sophia, 'and if she is fond of cats, is there any harm in it?'

Jane could make no answer, for by this time old Martha had seen them, and came halting on her crutch to meet them, and to offer them all the seats in her house; and these were only a three-legged stool and two old chairs.

Sophia then presented the old woman with what she had brought from her mamma, and Jane gave her a bottle of medicine from her pocket: and the old woman spoke of the goodness of Almighty God, who had put it into the lady's heart to provide her with what she needed most in this world.

Now, while Sophia and Jane and Martha were looking over the things which the lady had sent, the old cat had left the hob, and had come to Soffrona, and was staring wildly, and mewing in a strange way round the basket; and at the same time the kitten within began to mew. 'Puss! Puss! pretty Puss!' said Soffrona, for she was half afraid of this large cat, yet at the same time very well inclined to form a friendship with her.

At length, those that were with her in the cottage saw what was passing, and Martha said, 'Don't be afraid, Miss; Tibby won't hurt you. Poor thing! She is in great trouble, and has been so ever since yesterday.'

'What trouble?' said Soffrona.

'Some rude boys came in yesterday, and stole her kitten,' replied Martha. 'I was in the wood, picking a few sticks, and left the door open; and the boys came in, and ran away with the kitten; and the poor cat has been moaning and grieving like a human being – poor dumb thing – ever since. The cruel lads! I saw them go down the hill!'

'O!' said Soffrona, 'and I do believe—'

'And I am sure,' said Sophia.

'And I am so glad!' said Soffrona.

'And how happy she will be!' said Sophia.

And Soffrona immediately set down her basket and opened it, and put the little kitten on the floor, for the kitten was indeed poor Tibby's kitten.

It was a pretty sight, an agreeable and pleasant sight, to behold the joy of the old cat when she saw her kitten. The poor creature seemed as if she would have talked. Martha took up the kitten and laid it on a little bit of a mat in the corner of the chimney, where it used to be; and the old cat ran to it, and lay down by it, and gave it milk, and licked it, and talked to it in her way (that is, in the way that cats use to their kittens), and purred so loud, that you might have heard her to the very end of the cottage. It was a pleasant sight, as I said before, for it is a pleasure to see anything happy; and Soffrona jumped and capered about the house, and knew not how sufficiently to express her joy: and as for little Sophia, her eyes were filled with tears; and poor old Martha was not the least happy of the party.

And now, when it was time to go, Soffrona took up her empty basket, and giving the kitten a kiss, 'Little Puss,' she said, 'I will rejoice in your happiness, though it will be a loss to me, for I must part with my little darling. But I will not be selfish: Mamma says that I can never make myself happy by making other things miserable. Goodbye, little Puss: if God will help me, I will try never to be selfish.' And she walked out of the cottage, wiping away her tears.

'But you will let her have Muff, won't you, Martha,'

said Sophia, 'when her mother has brought her up, and can part with her?'

'To be sure I will, dear Miss,' replied Martha, 'for I was delighted to hear her say that she knew she never could make herself happy by making others miserable.'

When Muff was a quarter old, she was brought to Soffrona, and became her cat, and lived in her service till her yellow and black hairs were mingled with grey.

VARJAK PAW

by S. F. Said

When you write children's books and become rea-
sonably well known, journalists sometimes want to
interview you for their newspapers or magazines. This
is mostly enjoyable, because it's fun to talk about your
own book, but you have to be quite wary. Sometimes a
few unscrupulous journalists try to trick you to come
out with all kinds of comments and then twist what
you say.

I think my most delightful and interesting interview ever was with S. F. Said. He knew so much
about children's books and we found we had all sorts
of things in common – we even shared a passion for
gothic silver jewellery. He told me that he'd written a
children's book himself and so I asked him to send me
a copy when it came out.

I was thrilled when I read Varjak Paw. *It's new and contemporary and original, and yet it already reads like a true classic of children's literature.*

JWS

☙ VARJAK PAW ☙

Varjak awoke at the foot of the wall. His head was pounding, his paws aching. It wasn't quite light yet, but the night was almost over. The fall from the tree must have knocked him out. What a dream! He wondered if he'd ever have another like it.

He shivered. It was cold out in the open, and the grass beneath his body was wet. He stood up, shook the moisture from his fur, and looked around.

The view cleared his head instantly. Outside was like nothing he'd seen, or even dreamed of.

The Contessa's house stood on top of a high hill. Beneath it was a broad, green park. Beyond it, away in the distance, was a city.

Stretched out under the open sky, shining like silver in the pre-dawn light, the city was a huge, mad jumble of shapes and sizes. It had tall towers, gleaming steel and glass – but also squat brick houses, dark with chimney smoke. Wide open gardens jostled with narrow alleys; sharp pointy spires topped soft, curved domes; concrete blocks loomed over bright painted billboards.

They were all in there together, side by side, each one part of the whole. There was so much, he couldn't take it in. All he could hear from here was the wind rustling through the treetops, but down in the city it looked noisy and bustling, a place that never went to sleep.

His whiskers twitched with a mix of energy, excitement, danger. His heart beat faster, just looking at it. It seemed like a city where anything could happen, and probably did. A place you could do whatever you liked, and no one would stop you. Where you'd be able to find everything you wanted – even a dog.

The terror of the night before, the fight with the Gentleman's cats: it seemed a long time ago, and very far away. There was sadness in his heart for the Elder Paw, deep sadness, but his grandfather had trusted him with a mission. It was his duty as a Blue to save the family, and Varjak intended to see it through.

He ventured down the hill. It was steeper than it looked, and soon he found himself running, almost rolling down the slope. But it was a joy to stretch out in the open. A splash of sunshine lit the horizon. He'd never seen a sunrise before, and the sky Outside was alive with streaks of amber light.

The sky flashed past his eyes as he sped up, sprinted to the bottom. He bounded over a fence at the foot of the hill and into the park.

Around this time, back in the Contessa's house, the family would be waking up and licking each other clean. Varjak grinned. He hated washing, and already there was a satisfying build-up of mud between his claws.

Next, the family would obediently munch their food out of china bowls. It would be the Gentleman's vile-smelling caviare today. But now that he was Outside, he wouldn't have to eat anything he didn't like. He could choose what to eat and when to eat.

After eating, the family would go to their litter trays. Ha! Varjak crouched by a tree. No litter tray for him today. It felt good; it felt natural. It felt, he thought, like it ought to feel.

This was how it would be in the future. It was going to be the best time of his life. He'd return from the city with a dog (whatever a dog was) and defeat the Gentleman and his strange black cats. Then he'd lead his family out of that stuffy old house into this wonderful new world. They'd all say he was a proper Mesopotamian Blue, a true son of Jalal. They'd offer him every kind of honour and reward, but he'd turn them down. 'I did it for the glory of the family,' he'd say humbly, and they would cheer him even more.

Varjak wandered further and further in his happy daze. He barely noticed the fiery shades of sunrise burn out, leaving a sky the colour of cold ashes.

A violent sound cut through his thoughts. It was like a shrieking and roaring at the same time, and it scared him. The sound came from a black road that circled the park in the distance. He crept towards it, ears pressed against his skull. And then he saw them.

It was a column of fearsome monsters. They were rolling down the road, roaring at each other and everything around them. Huge monsters made of metal with sharp edges all around. They had yellow eyes at the front and red eyes at the back. They moved on round black wheels which turned so fast it made Varjak dizzy, and they belched a trail of choking smoke behind them on the wind.

Could these be dogs?

What were the Elder Paw's words? These monsters were big enough to kill a man. Their breath was
foul; their sound was deafening. And they filled his
heart with fear.

This was it. He was sure they were dogs. He'd
found them.

THE DIARY OF A KILLER CAT

by Anne Fine

Anne's the author of many prize-winning books, some very funny, some very serious. Her prose is always immaculate, every single word selected with unerring judgement. Anne once said she wrote all her stories with a pencil in a notebook, rubbing out each sentence until she'd got it exactly right. I don't know whether she still does, but her prose certainly reads like it.

Her Killer Cat books are wickedly funny – rather like Anne herself. She loves to tease. Wait till you read her comments about her own killer cat in the Pets' Corner section!

Jw

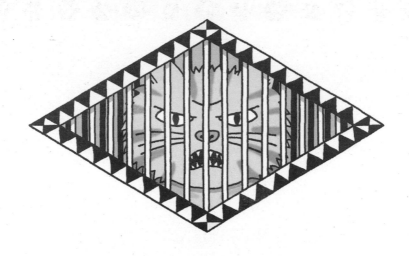

🐾 THE DIARY OF 🐾
A KILLER CAT

'Come out of there, you great fat furry psychopath. It's only a 'flu jab you're booked in for – more's the pity!'

Would *you* have believed him? I wasn't absolutely sure. (Neither was Ellie, so she tagged along.) I was still quite suspicious when we reached the vet's. That is *the only reason* why I spat at the girl behind the desk. There was no reason on earth to write HANDLE WITH CARE at the top of my case notes. Even the Thompsons' rottweiler doesn't have HANDLE WITH

CARE written on the top of his case notes. What's wrong with *me*?

So I was a little rude in the waiting room. So what? I *hate* waiting. And I especially hate waiting stuffed in a wire cat cage. It's cramped. It's hot. And it's boring. After a few hundred minutes of sitting there quietly, *anyone* would start teasing their neighbours. I didn't *mean* to frighten that little sick baby gerbil half to death. I was only *looking* at it. It's a free country, isn't it? Can't a cat even *look* at a sweet little baby gerbil?

And if I was licking my lips (which I wasn't) that's only because I was thirsty. Honestly. I wasn't trying to pretend I was going to eat it.

The trouble with baby gerbils is they can't take a *joke*.

And neither can anyone else round here.

Ellie's father looked up from the pamphlet he was reading called 'Your Pet and Worms'. (Oh, nice. Very nice.)

'Turn the cage round the other way, Ellie,' he said.

Ellie turned my cage round the other way.

Now I was looking at the Fishers' terrier. (And if there's any animal in the world who ought to have HANDLE WITH CARE written at the top of his case notes, it's the Fishers' terrier.)

OK, so I hissed at him. It was only a little hiss. You

practically had to have bionic ears to *hear* it.

And I did growl a bit. But you'd think he'd have a head start on growling. He is a dog, after all. I'm only a cat.

And yes, OK, I spat a bit. But only a bit. Nothing you'd even *notice* unless you were waiting to pick on someone.

Well, how was I to know he wasn't feeling very well? Not *everyone* waiting for the vet is ill. I wasn't ill, was I? Actually, I've never been ill in my life. I don't even know what it *feels* like. But I reckon, even if I were *dying*, something furry locked in a cage could make an eensy-weensy noise at me without my ending up whimpering and cowering, and scrabbling to get under the seat, to hide behind the knees of my owner.

More a *chicken* than a Scotch terrier, if you want my opinion.

'Could you please keep that vile cat of yours under control?' Mrs Fisher said nastily.

Ellie stuck up for me.

'He is in a cage!'

'He's still scaring half the animals in here to death. Can't you cover him up, or something?'

Ellie was going to keep arguing, I could tell. But without even looking up from his worm pamphlet, her father just dropped his raincoat over my cage as if I were some mangy old *parrot* or something.

And everything went black.

No wonder by the time the vet came at me with her nasty long needle, I was in a bit of a mood. I didn't mean to scratch her that badly, though.

Or smash all those little glass bottles.

Or tip the expensive new cat scales off the bench.

Or spill all that cleaning fluid.

It wasn't me who ripped my record card into tiny pieces, though. That was the vet.

When we left, Ellie was in tears again. (Some people are born soft.) She hugged my cage tightly to her chest.

'Oh, Tuffy! Until we find a new vet who'll promise to look after you, you must be so careful not to get run over.'

'Fat chance!' her father muttered.

I was just glowering at him through the cage wire, when he spotted Ellie's mother, standing knee-deep in shopping bags outside the supermarket.

'You're very late,' she scolded. 'Was there a bit of trouble at the vet's?'

PETS' CORNER

I've wanted to be a writer ever since I was six years old. As a child I read about authors with enormous interest. I especially liked reading about their own childhood, the books they'd liked to read themselves and, most of all, the pets they'd had.

So here's a special selection of favourite authors telling you all about their pets.

JW

🐾 TUFFY 🐾

Everyone loves Tuffy the Killer Cat, and I admit he is based on a pet we had for years and years. Usually we have huge and hairy Bernese mountain dogs, and I adore them. (I've always preferred a pet you bump into to one you trip over.)

But when we lived in California my younger daughter was so happy at school that she didn't want to come back to Britain. We had to bribe her to cheer up about the idea. 'As soon as we're back home, you can have a cat.'

She held us to the promise. The cat was pleasant enough with Cordelia, but it was foul with us. (I expect it knew that both Richard and I prefer dogs.) Richard disliked it even more than I did because he loves to garden and is fond of wildlife, and we all know what cats get up to in a freshly dug vegetable patch, and how they like to amuse themselves with vulnerable small creatures.

The years went by, and Cordelia went off to university, leaving us with this nasty-tempered and ungrateful beast. We did our best, but no one has ever been so glad to hear a vet say sadly, 'I'm afraid this cat is on a high road to Nowhere . . .'

The day Tuffy was put down, we shared a bottle of champagne and swore we'd never, ever have a cat again. (I'd rather leave a child behind in California!)

And the joke is that these Killer Cat books – there are six of them now – are popular in over twenty languages, and more each year. That horrid pet is now repaying us for all our pains by pretty well single-handedly earning my pension.

I feel quite fondly about Tuffy now.

Anne Fine

❧ OUR DOGS ❧

We have had three dogs and many more cats. The dogs had more vivid personalities, and I think I loved them more because of it. Our first dog was a lurcher whom we called Daisy. She had the most beautiful and kindly nature of any animal I've known. Once, when a friend of ours was terribly unhappy, she (the friend) was sitting on our sofa and she began to cry. Daisy came and laid her head on the friend's knee in a gesture that could only mean deep sympathy.

We also had two pugs, a brother and sister. He, Hoagy, was black, and Nellie was fawn, the colour that most pugs are. Their hair felt different: hers was coarser than his, which was very soft, like cashmere.

I have never known such stupid creatures. They were absolutely untrainable. Whatever we tried to teach them to do, whether to sit, to come to us, to stand still, all they would do when we called was turn and look at us blankly, and then carry on with whatever they were doing.

But they bore out what I've noticed about human siblings: just because they were born to the same mother and father, that didn't mean that they were similar in character. Hoagy was languid (idle, frankly) and perfectly genial. He would roll over on his back and allow himself to be tickled with no fear or hesitation. Nellie was the exact opposite. I don't think she ever rolled over on her back in her entire life. What she thought was going to happen if she did, I don't like to speculate, but she would squirm and wriggle and do anything to get away. You could feel a sort of nervous tension in all her muscles when you picked her up, whereas Hoagy would lie in your arms with no more animation than a beanbag.

We loved them all, of course, and did our best to keep them healthy. However, Hoagy got fatter and fatter, and we couldn't work out why. Finally we saw him crawling back under the fence from the next door garden, and realized that he'd been visiting the students who lived there. When we asked them about

it, they said, 'Yes, he's a great eater. He'll eat anything except Marmite.' They must have been feeding
him for months.

The only thing that makes living with a dog less
than an ideal relationship is that their lives are so
much shorter than ours, and we have to arrange for
their deaths when they get old and ill. That's almost
too painful to be borne, but we have to do it.

We haven't got a dog at the moment, and I have
to say that life is a lot easier: we can go away at a
moment's notice without having to find somewhere
for the dog to stay. But I wouldn't be surprised if we
had another dog one day.

Philip Pullman

❧ PEKINGESE ❧

Years ago, on my sixteenth birthday, I was given five pounds to buy a Persian kitten. Most girls pine for an animal of their own but, even as a little child, for me the longing was not just for an animal but for an extraordinary animal; I would have loved a unicorn rather than a pony, if there had really been unicorns, or a salamander, or a kylin – that mythical monster with the head of a lion and the body of a dragon – if I had known about them, but a Persian kitten was the nearest my dear family could come to fulfilling this unusual wish.

In the pet shop there was a rusty old bird-cage and in it sat a puppy, small, square, black with cream paws and vest; he was of a kind I had not seen before, but his eyes, that took up most of his face, looked at me compellingly. I bought him, my five pounds was accepted as a down-payment with a pledge of half a crown a week from my allowance for a year.

I am sure now that the shopkeeper did not expect me to come back as, in pekingese parlance, this puppy was flawed; for one thing his lower jaw protruded, a fault the Chinese call 'earth covers heaven', so that he was worth precisely nothing – to anybody else; but I am glad now that I met every one of those Saturday morning extortions so that my lifetime of pekingese – I have had more than twenty – was founded on fidelity, however slight. I called the puppy Piers because it was the most aristocratic name I could think of.

In those days, though I had an ignoramus's love of things Chinese, poetry, ceramics and paintings, I knew nothing of the dynasties and their emperors and empresses; of palace cities and paeony-terraced ten-mile-wide gardens; of eunuchs and concubines; of the silk caravan route or of opium clippers. I knew practically nothing either of Queen Victoria and Court life at Windsor, Balmoral and Buckingham Palace; of treaties and wars and, if I had, would not have dreamed of connecting them with pekingese. I only knew Piers but my instinct was right – no matter how flawed, Piers by origin was aristocratic – more, he was Imperial.

It may seem absurd to link a race of small dogs with two vast empires, one Western, the other Far Eastern and, in particular, with the two powerful women who, in the nineteenth century, ruled over them, but no one can follow the story of the pekingese without some knowledge of these two utterly different and distant worlds.

The Chinese regarded Westerners as vandals and there is certainly something unthinking and prejudiced in the image of this blithe and historic breed we have conjured up and, sadly, often made fact: that of rich ladies' lapdogs, pampered and delicate, dressed in coats, bad-tempered, even snappy, wheezing, snoring and so adipose they can only waddle. If they have been distorted into this, the fault lies with the owner, not with the dog. True, elderly people buy them believing they need little exercise – which is wrong; most pekingese detest laps, are even wary of fondling, are only bad-tempered through being made liverish from too many tidbits. It is true, too, that they snore, but that is because of what man, through the ages, has done to their noses, and the snores are usually only a soporific snuffle. As for waddling! Pekingese can race, even hurdle; they retrieve, swim and are more hardy

than many a big dog, walking in any weather; sometimes in snow or deluging rain my pekingese have
been the only dogs out in the woods or on the hills.

Most of us dog-owners are ordinary people and
so most pekingese nowadays have to settle not for
palaces, but for an ordinary humdrum life, but they
still treat it in a lordly way. Piers, for instance, soon
became a well-known character in our Sussex town.
'In quod again', a policeman would come to our door
and say, and I would have to go to the police station
and redeem Piers with a fine of five shillings. The
trouble was that while I was away at school he was
bored and so would slip out; and kind people, seeing
a small pekingese wandering alone, thought he was
lost. By no means: a bus ran from a stop near our
then house up to the Downs; one morning I caught
it with Piers, meaning to take him for a walk on the
rolling green hills – it should have been a chariot or
imperial cart or, at least, a car, but for us it had to
be a bus. 'That your dog, Miss?' asked the conductor.
'Well, I guess you owe the Corporation at least five
pounds.' It seems that Piers caught the bus in the
morning, took himself off to the front seat on the top
– buses were open-topped then – alighted at the ter-
minus at the foot of the Downs and went rabbiting
and, at the right time, caught the bus home. I had

long been puzzled by the earth on his paws and ruff.

He became my shadow, mourning if I went anywhere without him, making a carnival of joy of my return; alert to every word I said, sensitive to every mood, but after twenty halcyon months we went back to India and I had to leave him. I never saw him again.

Rumer Godden

❀ MIMI'S DAY ❀

Our cat, Mimi, who was always known as Meems, lived with us from 1990 to 2004. She was a tabby cat with one white shoulder, and my husband described her perfectly as the kind of creature you can imagine with a handbag in the crook of her arm. She was elegant and beautiful, like very many cats, but had about her an air of femininity and sweetness that was quite unusual. The fierceness sometimes associated with tabby cats was completely missing from her looks and her character. She was the very opposite of a hunter. She'd crouch on the step and look in a meaningful way at squirrels racing past her nose without ever chasing any of them. She never once in fourteen years brought in a mouse or a bird, for which we were very grateful. Some people said the reason she never hunted was because we spoiled her rotten, but I don't believe that . . . I think the hunting instinct is something a cat either has or doesn't. Still, it's true she was pampered. She had dry food and wet food and water out for her pleasure every day. She was never left in a cattery, and indeed for the time we had her, my husband and I took separate holidays so that Meems wouldn't have to be on her own, even for one night. We thought of her as one of the family and loved her very much. When she died, of an illness that we could no longer get treatment for, we were bereft. I kept seeing her out of the corner of my eye in every part of the house for a very long time. We think of her often and remember her with delight and pleasure. She was a loving and lap-sitting cat, and not one of the standoffish kind. I'm really pleased to think that people will be able to read about her now. Here's a poem I wrote about her.

From her position on the windowsill
she gives the garden her consideration.
Later, both the camellias and the ferns
will undergo a full investigation.

First, she will be a small domestic sphinx
unmoving on the carpet, enigmatic,
thinking: there was a fire here last night
and now it's gone. All life is problematic.

The second serious question of the day
is: where to sleep? Which bed or chair to grace?
The velvet spaces of the chesterfield?
Or should she seek a woolly resting place?

They sometimes leave (she thinks) jerseys on beds,
or there's a shawl spread softly on a chair.
Also a cupboard full of fluffy towels
and gurgling darkness . . . maybe she'll go there.

She steps into the garden after lunch:
a meal she'd hoped might magically be prawns
but wasn't. She is philosophical.
It is the hour for stalking things on lawns.

Squirrels are jet-propelled and every bird
annoyingly decides to fly away.
She races up a tree trunk, just to show
she might catch something, on some other day.

❧ MIMI'S DAY ❧

And meanwhile, she'll adopt a watchful pose
on a convenient step, warm in the sun,
until her head grows heavy, droops and falls.
The work of sleepy cats is never done.

The moths come out at night. Then she's awake.
Their grey and blurring wings catch on her claws.
When they are still, she stretches bends and yawns
and with a sharp pink tongue, tidies her paws.

Adèle Geras

✿ PETS I HAVE HAD ✿

All children like pets, especially, of course, dogs and cats, and even better than those they like puppies and kittens. I only had one pet as a child, and that was a kitten who was sent away after I had had it for a fortnight. I was heart-broken. I called it Chippy, I don't know why, and I used to rush home from school to play with it.

My mother was not very fond of animals. My father loved all wild animals and birds, but he was not interested in dogs or cats because he loved his garden so much. He couldn't bear to think of animals rushing over his beautiful patches of violets, or breaking his delphiniums.

So my brothers and I never had any pets at all, and I used to spend much of my time playing with the kittens and puppies belonging to friends of mine. If you love animals you have got to be with them somehow, even if you haven't any of your own.

I kept caterpillars though, but they were not allowed in the house. I had to keep them at the bottom of the garden in a shed. I couldn't *love* my caterpillars, though I liked them, and never forgot to feed them, and I liked feeling their funny clingy feet walking over my hand. The only caterpillars I really liked immensely were the furry 'woolly-bear' ones – you know the kind I mean. You can stroke them. They are the hairy caterpillars of the tiger-moth and are lovely things.

I couldn't *love* caterpillars because it seemed rather a waste of love when they were going to stop being caterpillars and turn into something else. That really did seem like magic to me. I used to try very hard to be there when the chrysalis split open and out came a moth or a butterfly with limp and draggled wings.

'I will have all the cats and dogs and birds and fish I want when I am grown-up,' I said to myself. 'If I have to save for a year I'll buy a dog of my own. And if I have children when I am grown-up and married, they shall have all the pets they want.'

That's one of the nice things about being a child —
if you haven't got something you badly want you can
always plan to have it when you are grown-up. And
if you are determined enough you *do* get it, though
it usually means working very hard. But things are
much more precious to you if you have to work for
them, and seem much more worth-while then than if
you just have them given to you.

Well, of course, when I was grown-up, I did get pets
of my own; all kinds, from dogs and cats to goldfish
and hedgehogs!

First I had a dog called Bobs. He was a handsome
smooth-haired fox-terrier with a fine head. He was
very clever indeed. If I said 'Die for the King, Bobs!'
he would at once roll over and pretend to be dead.
And there he would lie, perfectly still, till I said
'Come alive!' Then he would jump up and look for the
biscuit he always got when he was a clever dog!

He could shut the door for me too. Not only that
but he would listen for the 'click' of the door, to make
sure it was properly shut. He could sit up and trust,
of course, even when a biscuit was balanced on his
nose. I had him for years, a faithful companion,
merry and intelligent.

Then I had a wife for him, an amusing little smooth-haired terrier called Sandy. Sandy was white with a sandy-coloured head, and she was a dear, affectionate little dog. The two of them lived in a little dog-house together. It had two doors, a partition between the two rooms, and a bench in each room, raised from the floor. Here Sandy had many beautiful puppies, so Gillian and Imogen, my two children, grew up always surrounded by dogs.

I had more fox-terriers after that, and the last was Topsy, a funny little dog with a black head, and just about the smallest brain I should think any dog ever had. You will see how queer she was when you hear the following story!

One day my children thought they would like to keep mice. So they bought some, and took them up to the nursery. They put the mice on a high book-case, out of Topsy's way.

Topsy saw them running about in their cage, of course, and she sat down in front of the book-case and watched them for hours.

We thought it was silly of Topsy to sit and stare like that for hours and as the mice smelt rather strongly, I took the cage down to the verandah and put it there, where the mice were very happy. I put a clock on the book-case in the place where the mice had been.

Topsy sat for hours and stared at the clock! We

never could make out what she thought – whether she thought the mice had turned into the clock, or lived inside it, or what!

Anyway we really couldn't bear to see Topsy staring steadfastly at the clock all day long, so we put it on the mantel-piece and then there was nothing on the book-case at all. But dear old Topsy still sat there, staring at nothing for hours and hours! She really was an absurd little dog.

Then one day she got into the garden next door and, for some extraordinary reason, killed nineteen hens and chicks – so we had to send poor Topsy away to someone who lived in a town, where there were no hens near. We were all very sad.

Then I had a dear little dog called Lassie, a black cocker spaniel. And now I have Laddie, also a spaniel, who appears in many of my books as Loony. We often think that Loony would be a better name for him than Laddie, because he really *is* such a lunatic sometimes!

He fetches all the mats and the cushions and some of the towels, and drapes them about the house – in the hall is one of his favourite places! He sometimes goes completely mad and tears up and down the stairs and round and round the rooms at top speed. Yes, Loony would certainly be a better name for him!

❧ PETS I HAVE HAD ❧

I couldn't tell you how many cats and kittens I have had since I was grown up. I love Siamese cats, with their creamy coats, dark brown points and strange, brilliant blue eyes. I bred them for years, and many a time I have had as many as ten or twelve small Siamese kittens racing about, plaguing the life out of Bobs or Sandy. They are most amusing, and are really more like dogs than cats.

They look a bit like monkeys, they act rather like squirrels in the way they sit up and hold things, they have some of the nature of a dog – and yet they are cats! What a peculiar mixture! The one I have now, Bimbo, licks me like a dog, and follows me about like a dog too.

He will go after a little ball and bring it back in his mouth. I say 'Drop it!' and he drops it for me to throw. He will hunt for anything I have hidden till he finds it. He is really beautiful.

I have had other cats, of course – tabby ones – a magnificent ginger one called Rufus – a black one with white socks. But Bimbo is the cleverest of them all.

Enid Blyton

❀ MY PETS ❀

Sometimes I think the ages of our lives have been defined by the pets who came to live with us. So childhood was a goldfish I won at a country fair, called Swimsy. She/he swam around the bowl mesmorisingly and went barracuda-line at feeding time. So we fed him/her a lot.

When Swimsy died we got a dog. Prynne was a retriever-cross-Labrador with long floppy ears, who slobbered wonderfully.

Married life began with a Shetland sheepdog called Puck who was wild about everything and quite tiring. Katie, a beautiful Irish setter, smiled through her life. She loved us completely, and loved her puppies even more – Arthur, Hal and Galadriel.

Next came Sophie, an English setter with mournful eyes and a heart of gold. She was wonderful with our children and grandchildren; she slept as contentedly as she lived and she lived long. And our last dog, Bercelet, a rescue lurcher, was the love of my wife's life. She barely tolerated me, the dog, I mean. She barked rarely and ate minimally. She ran like the wind, loved the wind too. Wind suited her, but she was a fragile, tender creature, and died suddenly, which left us bereft.

We've had cats too in our time. Snug and Bottom, both kittens born in the wild (quite Shakespearean, the names we chose in those days). Then Mini, Simpson, Leo – a beautiful neurotic Abyssinian – but when we had cats we had no birds in the garden. Now we have no cats and hundreds of birds, and five goldfish swimming in and out of the weeds in our pond, every one a Swimsy. I'm back where I began, second childhood.

We long for another dog, which is maybe why dogs appear so often in my stories, in *Shadow* (a spaniel), *Born to Run* (a greyhound), *Cool* (a Jack Russell terrier), *The Last Wolf* (a wolf), and many others. As for cats, I put them in my books too, that way they don't kill birds! So we still have dogs and cats a-plenty, if you see what I'm saying.

Michael Morpurgo

☙ DOG MEMORY ☙

When I was eight or nine we had a German shepherd called Tarquis. He had beautiful, sleek, golden brown and black fur, a strong body and a beautiful, wolfish face. And he was *huge*, but with a very gentle nature. Every afternoon after school, I'd take him for a walk in our local park. I loved walking with him next to me; he was so tall and I was so small, but next to him I felt very tall indeed.

One afternoon, after we reached the park, I let Tarquis off his lead and chucked a ball for him to chase. Time and time again, he chased after the ball, tail wagging, before grabbing it in his jaws and bringing it back to me. Lots of other people were in the park also exercising their dogs. There was one dog in particular, a Yorkshire terrier, or Yorkie, which was chasing around like it was demented.

So, for about the tenth time, I chucked my tennis ball and Tarquis chased after it. The only trouble was, the Yorkie chased after it too. The Yorkie snatched up the ball in its mouth and ran off with it. Tarquis chased the dog across the park, and both dogs were at full stretch. The Yorkie's owner was shouting at me to call my dog to heel. But then the Yorkie turned, dropped the ball and chased after Tarquis.

Tarquis turned and legged it. He ran for his life. The Yorkie was a toy dog, barely thirty centimetres high. Tarquis was huge, at least three times as long and three times as high, yet he ran like his life depended on it. And all the other dog owners around me roared with laughter.

Yes, it was embarrassing, especially when Tarquis slunk back to me with his tail between his legs and without my ball – which I had to get myself!

Tarquis is long gone, but every time I recall that incident it makes me smile. Tarquis really was a gentle giant, and thanks to him I've always had a love of German shepherd dogs. Never been terribly keen on Yorkies though! Just goes to show that bullies come in all shapes and sizes.

Malorie Blackman

❧ MY ANIMAL FRIENDS ❧

Nanny Anna

People think that a dachshund is just a sort of short-legged, long-bodied dog. They do not realize that there are dogs . . . and there are dachshunds.

Dogs like to please their owners by doing what they are told. Dachshunds like to please themselves.

Our first ever dachshund was called Anna, and when we got her as a puppy, she took not the slightest notice of anything we said to her.

'She must be stone deaf,' we said. But she wasn't. She was just a dachshund.

Apart from being as stubborn as all her breed,

Anna's speciality was mother-love. Quite early in her life she began to be called Nanny.

It wasn't just her own puppies that she fussed over. She did not need to be in milk, she just came into it at the drop of a baby. Kittens were well received if there was a cat crisis. And once she tried to play mother to four piglets.

A young sow had rejected them, but Nanny thought that they were lovely and immediately settled down to nurse them in her basket. Alas, newborn piglets, unlike puppies, have sharp little teeth, but still Anna put up with them till they could be fostered on to another sow. She saved their lives, in fact.

Dodo: Star of the Show

Our miniature red wire-haired dachshund, Dodo, was born on a farm in west Wales, and from the moment we picked her up to bring her home with us, it was plain that she was a most unusual dog.

Though so young and so small, she was very self-possessed. The first of our animals that she met was a Great Dane. He bent his huge head to this midget. She looked up and wagged at him.

Some years later, when Dodo was about five, something happened that changed her life.

A television producer was looking for a presenter for a small slot on a children's programme. She needed someone who had been a farmer and a teacher and wrote books for children (that turned out to be me), and who also owned a small, attractive dog (that was Dodo).

Dodo and I must have made about fifty little films.

Though I improved as time went on, Dodo didn't need to: she was immediately at home in front of the cameras. Not only did she like people, so that she always got on very well with the film crews, but she was always extremely likeable herself.

At first, the crew came often to our cottage, for we filmed a number of animals there or near by, and they always arrived promptly at nine o'clock on a Thursday morning.

By a quarter to nine each Thursday (and only on Thursday), Dodo would be waiting by the door for them to arrive and admire her.

Don't ask me how she knew. I don't know.

After a while Dodo began to be recognized in public. In London once, I suddenly heard some children crying, 'Look! It's Dodo!' and they rushed up and made a fuss of her, which she loved; not because she was vain but because she was always so friendly to everyone.

And it wasn't only children who recognized her.

The guard of an Intercity train once came to punch my ticket (and hers).

'Why,' he said, 'if it isn't Dodo!'

She was always the star of the show.

Postscript

Remember Dodo, the star of the show? It might be nice, I'm thinking now, to end with a mention of another miniature red wire-haired dachshund called Little Elsie, who is sitting watching me.

Why? Because Little Elsie is Dodo's grand-daughter.

She's quite a different character from her granny – not as jolly and outgoing, less sure of herself (though she's as fierce as a lion when left in charge of the car); in fact not the filmstar type.

But the older Little Elsie grows – and she's really quite old now, though still very active – the more she gets to look like her grandmother. Her red coat has paled with age, her beard and moustache are fuller, her muzzle is grey.

And lately a funny thing has begun to happen. We keep calling Elsie by the wrong name. Several times a day, one or other of us will say, 'Come along, Dodo,' and along comes Little Elsie, wagging her tail and doing her special trick, which is to bare her teeth in a grin of pleasure.

Dick King-Smith

❧ CATS ❧

Real cats, of course, vary in their natures just as much as humans do. I have met spiteful cats, loving cats, clever cats, stupid cats. A highly intelligent orange cat, January, who adopted my father one New Year's Day, learned how to rattle the latch of the dining-room door, so that it would swing open and let him in. He also, all by himself, invented a charming trick: when you softly clapped your hands above his head, he would lift up his right front paw to be shaken. Then there was Gracchus, a tabby belonging to my sister, who used to come and stay at our house along with my two nieces for summer holidays. He was epileptic and had to be given a tiny pill every day. This aroused great feelings of jealousy in our cat Hamlet, who thought he was missing out on some treat – so terrific dexterity and diplomacy were needed to get the pill into the right cat. And then there was Darwin, dear Darwin, who always took a shortcut through the banisters, and liked to lie with his shaggy arms around one's neck . . .

Joan Aiken

❧ SHANTI ❧

We almost didn't choose Shanti, who was one of a litter of three Tibetan spaniel puppies. She and her sisters were rolling around together, then Shanti trotted over to my son Josh, climbed on his lap and peed on him. Josh, then, was very put out. We sponged his trousers and the breeder dried him off with a hair-dryer. One puppy ran into the crate and cowered. Her sister froze. Shanti ignored it. 'This is the puppy for you,' said her breeder. 'She's calm and will do well in a house with children.'

Pauline was right. Shanti is only frightened of other dogs. Not fireworks, not hoovers, not loud bangs.

❧ SHANTI ❧

We got Shanti the first term Josh entered secondary school, thirteen years ago. I fell in love with the breed, which is an ancient one, leafing through a dog encyclopaedia. I'd never seen a Tibbie before, as they are rare in the UK. Shanti has this solemn, furrowed, almost quizzical face, and I loved her lion-like golden mane, and the fact that even today, as an elderly pooch, she still looks a lot like a puppy.

Shanti is well-known in our north London neighbourhood, as she likes sitting in the front window on top of the sofa, and watching people pass by. Her other favourite place is inside her 'Shanti box', a cardboard box my husband made for her, with a little square entrance hole. We used to get through one a week when she was a puppy, as she loved destroying them from the inside. We were delighted, however, as it meant she never chewed on furniture or shoes.

Shanti adores being with people. If we have friends round, we always pull up a chair for her, as she likes being part of a circle. She's the perfect writer's dog, as she sleeps (and snores) beneath my desk while I work.

However, Shanti would never win any prizes for

obedience. She's quite headstrong and only obeys if she feels like it. Which is not very often.

Shanti has been part of my son's childhood. Now he is grown up, and she is old. I look at her, with her slippy hind legs and her white muzzle, and can't believe how fast our time has gone.

Francesca Simon

❄ MY PETS ❄

Cats and dogs make wonderful companions. We have nine of them! Three cats and six dogs, all rescues. The cats are Thomas, Titch and Bella. The dogs are Dolly, Daisy, Minnie, Gertie, Benny and Sasha.

To start with, like most people, we had just one dog. A little fox terrier. And like most people we bought her from a breeder. It didn't occur to us to go to Battersea or one of the other rescue centres. On the other hand, we have never gone to a breeder for a cat. Neither of us had ever lived with cats and never thought of having one, until one day we were adopted by a small tabby, who simply arrived on the doorstep and took up residence. She showed no fear whatsoever of the fox terrier. If anything, it was the fox terrier who trembled! What was this strange thing, invading her space? We put up notices on trees and lampposts – FOUND: SMALL TABBY CAT – but no one ever claimed her, so there we were, one cat, one dog. The fox terrier had her own special chair and we held our breath when, one momentous day, the cat decided to jump up and settle next to her. But no problems! The chair became 'their chair' and they spent many happy hours cuddled up together.

In time we decided we would like a second dog, but by now we knew about rescue organizations, so off we went to one that was local to us. People say, 'Oh, but it would break my heart to see all those poor animals desperate for a home! How can you bear to do it?' It's not easy, I'll admit. More difficult, perhaps, with dogs than with cats, since cats tend to sit in silent resigna-tion, whereas a dog will come to the front of the cage and jump up and beg you to take it. But if you love animals, you have to remind yourself that if everyone said, 'Oh, it would break my heart,' then none of them would ever find new homes. And to help a confused and lonely cat or dog blossom and regain confidence is incredibly rewarding.

When we finally lost our little tabby cat we adopted two brothers, Smudger and Humphrey.

They were pure white, and Humphrey was deaf. He was the most affectionate cat I have ever known, and Smudger was without doubt the kindest. He looked after his brother with total devotion.

One of our earliest dogs came from Battersea. I vividly remember taking her home on the train, cuddling all the way. She was a very precious little person. Our first Daisy. A small black mongrel, seven years old, and a dear, sweet, zany little creature. Present-day Daisy is also a bit zany. She is a Jack Russell, who has to be kept on an expanding lead when out walking as she simply cannot trust herself not to go rushing off after interesting smells or disappearing down holes. Despite that, she spends half the walk fervently clutching at you, just to make sure you are still there. She was found wandering along a main road, so maybe she is scared of getting lost again.

Dolly is also a Jack Russell. She is a very girly little person. Too pretty for her own good! She fawns on any man who comes to the house, pawing at them and going all soft and melty. As a feminist, I sometimes feel quite ashamed of her . . .

Minnie *thinks* that she is a Jack Russell, and we haven't the heart to tell her she is just a 'small terrier type'. Our local rescue group insisted she was a little angel, and she certainly has the most immense charm. She wriggles and giggles and whirrs her paws to get your attention. But angel she is not! She makes a very naughty nuisance of herself with cats, who mostly sit about on high surfaces looking down at her with contempt. Stupid dawg!

Gertie is a tiny dish rag of a dog. Maybe a bit of Yorkie, maybe a bit of Norfolk terrier. Who knows? She is extremely cute and very fierce. Even the local rottweilers turn tail and run when they see Gertie approaching.

Sasha is a springer spaniel. She was seven when we adopted her, and fat as a barrel. It is horrible, and extremely cruel, when people let their dogs put on so much weight. Fortunately, after being with us for a few months she slimmed right down, and now, at the ripe age of fifteen, she still looks like a young dog. She is very keen that everyone should know she is the Only Pedigree in the Pack. Jack Russells, she says, with a well-bred sniff, are only *types*.

Benny, our one dog in a family of females, is a German shepherd/collie cross. A big, gentle, goofy boy, very laid-back and good-natured. He came from Wales, where he had been rounded up as a stray and was going to be put down. We lost our hearts the minute we saw him looking so eager in his cage at the rescue centre. Impossible to resist!

The cats all came from our local rescue lady, just up the road. There is stripy Tom, who won't put up with any nonsense from the annoying Minnie. There is Bella, who loves to purr and sit on a lap. And there is big black Titch, who as a kitten used to look like a tiny spider scuttling about the place. It was Bella who took him under her wing, mothering him and caring for him. And how did he repay her? For ages he ignored her, or even told her to stay away. It was like he and Tom were a sort of boys' club, and females weren't welcome. Now, however, they all curl up together – on our bed, naturally!

The cats sleep on the bed during the day, the dogs sleep on it at night. Well, three of them do. Minnie, Dolly and Daisy. And actually they don't sleep *on* it, so much as *in* it. They spend the night humpling about under the duvet, snuffling and twitching as they dream about walks. The other three have their own bed in the corner of the room. Gertie likes to burrow under a blanket. Sasha snores. Benny usually collapses with a big contented sigh onto a rug. If you get out of bed in the night, you tend to trip over him.

The cats are banished to two rooms at the back of the house. If we leave them roaming about, they thunder up and down the stairs like a herd of cavalry, or come banging and rattling at the bedroom door. If they are actually let *into* the bedroom, they jump on top of wardrobes or roam about on the mantelshelf, deliberately knocking things over. Or, even worse, they prink and poke at the dogs under the duvet, and Jack Russells then start springing about all over the place.

Oh, there is never a dull moment! But really, these little creatures ask so little. Just love, and shelter; and, for dogs, a daily walk. And food, of course. That goes without saying. Mustn't forget the food! Meal times are extremely important in an animal's life. Just as animals are extremely important in mine. They are truly, truly rewarding, and such loyal and loving friends. I couldn't live without them!

Jean Ure

DOG STORIES

THE INCREDIBLE JOURNEY

by Sheila Burnford

Ask your gran or grandad if they've ever seen a film called The Incredible Journey. *I bet they'll smile and start murmuring about old Bodger and his friends. It was an extraordinarily popular Walt Disney film in the 1960s – a story of two dogs and a cat trekking three hundred miles through rough Canadian country-side to find their way home. Bodger is an elderly white bull terrier, Luath is a strong young Labrador, and Tao is a sleek Siamese cat.*

The film was based on a bestselling book by Sheila Burnford. It's a very exciting and moving story, but it always seemed a little unlikely to me. I could just about believe that two dogs might somehow be able to find their way home – but would they seriously be

accompanied by a cat? I don't know how they trained the animals in the film, but they made a remarkably successful job of it. Bodger and Luath battled bravely, even fighting off a bear and a porcupine – and the cat playing Tao 'acted' her little heart out, even half drowning herself in a river. I have no idea how they made that lovely cat perform in such an extraordinary way. I can't even make Jacob and Lily come for their supper if they're happily playing in the garden.

I've included the last scene of the book. It's hard to read it and stay dry-eyed – and you definitely need a hankie if you watch a DVD of the old film. It all seems a bit corny and old-fashioned now, but the ending is still powerful enough to have me in floods of tears.

Jw

🐾 THE INCREDIBLE 🐾 JOURNEY

Everyone was silent and preoccupied. Suddenly Elizabeth stood up. 'Listen!' she said. 'Listen, Daddy – I can hear a dog barking!' Complete and utter silence fell as everyone strained their ears in the direction of the hills behind. No one heard anything.

'You're imagining things,' said her mother. 'Or perhaps it was a fox. Come along, we must start back.'

'Wait, wait! Just one minute – you'll be able to hear it in a minute, too,' whispered Elizabeth, and her mother, remembering the child's hearing was still young and acute enough to hear the squeaking noise of bats and other noises lost for ever to adults – and now even to Peter – remained silent.

Elizabeth's tense, listening expression changed to a slowly dawning smile. 'It's Luath!' she announced matter-of-factly. 'I know his bark!'

'Don't do this to us, Liz,' said her father gently, disbelieving. 'It's . . .'

Now Peter thought he heard something too: 'Shhh . . .'

There was silence again, everyone straining to hear in an agony of suspense. Nothing was heard. But Elizabeth had been so convinced, the knowledge written so plainly on her face, that now Jim Hunter experienced a queer, urgent expectancy, every nerve in his body tingling with certain awareness that something was going to happen. He rose and hurried down the narrow path to where it joined the broader track leading around the hill. 'Whistle, Dad!' said Peter breathlessly, behind him.

The sound rang out piercingly shrill and sweet, and almost before the echo rebounded a joyous, answering bark rang around the surrounding hills.

They stood there in the quiet afternoon, their taut bodies awaiting the relief of suspense; they stood at the road's end, waiting to welcome a weary traveller who had journeyed so far, with such faith, along it.

They had not long to wait.

Hurtling through the bushes on the high hillside of the trail a small, black-tipped wheaten body leaped the last six feet down with careless grace and landed softly at their feet. The unearthly, discordant wail of a welcoming Siamese rent the air.

Elizabeth's face was radiant with joy. She kneeled, and picked up the ecstatic, purring cat. 'Oh, Tao!' she said softly, and as she gathered him into her arms he wound his black needle-tipped paws lovingly around her neck. 'Tao!' she whispered, burying her nose in his soft, thyme-scented fur, and Tao tightened his grip in such an ecstasy of love that Elizabeth nearly choked.

Longridge had never thought of himself as being a particularly emotional man, but when the Labrador appeared an instant later, a gaunt, stare-coated shadow of the beautiful dog he had last seen, running as fast as his legs would carry him towards his master, all his soul shining out of sunken eyes, he felt a lump in his throat, and at the strange, inarticulate half-strangled noises that issued from the dog when he leaped at his master, and the expression on his friend's face, he had to turn away and pretend to loosen Tao's too loving paws.

Minutes passed; everyone had burst out talking

and chattering excitedly, gathering around the dog to stroke and pat and reassure, until he too threw every vestige of restraint to the winds, and barked as if he would never stop, shivering violently, his eyes alight and alive once more and never leaving his master's face. The cat, on Elizabeth's shoulder, joined in with raucous howls; everyone laughed, talked or cried at once, and for a while there was pandemonium in the quiet wood.

Then, suddenly – as though the same thought had struck them all simultaneously – there was silence. No one dared to look at Peter. He was standing aside, aimlessly cracking a twig over and over again until it became a limp ribbon in his hands. He had not touched Luath, and turned away now when the dog at last came over, including him in an almost human round of greeting.

'I'm glad he's back, Dad,' was all he said. 'And your old Taocat, too!' he added to Elizabeth, with a diffi-cult smile. Elizabeth, the factual, the matter-of-fact, burst into tears. Peter scratched Tao behind the ears, awkward, embarrassed. 'I didn't expect anything else – I told you that. I tell you what,' the boy continued, with a desperate cheerfulness, avoiding the eyes of his family, 'you go down – I'll catch up with you later. I want to go back to the Lookout and see if I can get a decent picture of that whisky-jack.'

There will never be a more blurred picture of a whisky-jack, said Uncle John grimly to himself. On an impulse he spoke aloud.

'How about if I came too, Peter? I could throw the crumbs and perhaps bring the bird nearer?' Even as he spoke he could have bitten back the words, expecting a rebuff, but to his surprise the boy accepted his offer.

They watched the rest of the family wending their way down the trail, Tao still clutched in Elizabeth's arms, gentle worshipping Luath restored at last to the longed-for position at his master's heels.

The two remaining now returned to Lookout Point. They took some photographs. They prised an odd-shaped fungus growth off a tree. They found, incredibly, the cylindrical core of a diamond drill. And all the time they talked: they talked of rockets, orbits, space; gravely they pondered the seven stomachs of a cow; tomorrow's weather; but neither mentioned dogs.

Now, still talking, they were back at the fork of the trail; Longridge looked surreptitiously at his watch: it was time to go. He looked at Peter. 'We'd better g—' he started to say, but his voice trailed off as he saw the expression on the face of the tense, frozen boy beside him, then followed the direction of his gaze . . .

Down the trail, out of the darkness of the bush and into the light of the slanting bars of sunlight, jogging along with his peculiar nautical roll, came – Ch. Boroughcastle Brigadier of Doune.

Boroughcastle Brigadier's ragged banner of a tail streamed out behind him, his battle-scarred ears were upright and forward, and his noble pink and black nose twitched, straining to encompass all that his short gaze was denied. Thin and tired, hopeful, happy – and hungry, his remarkable face alight with expectation – the old warrior was returning from the wilderness. Bodger, beautiful for once, was coming as fast as he could.

He broke into a run, faster and faster, until the years fell away, and he hurled himself towards Peter.

And as he had never run before, as though he would outdistance time itself, Peter was running towards his dog.

OSBERT

by Noel Streatfeild

Noel Streatfeild was one of my favourite authors when I was young. I've collected copies of her books for years. You might have read her brilliant book Ballet Shoes *or perhaps seen special reprints of* The Circus is Coming *or* White Boots *or* Tennis Shoes. *They're all fantastic family stories aimed at eight-to-twelve-year-olds – but she also wrote occasional books for younger children.*

I like a quirky little book about a dog called Osbert. He's a black poodle – but his hair has forgotten to curl. I love his special shaggy look, but he's considered not smart enough to go to a stylish wedding with his family. However, Monsieur Toto, the ladies' hairdresser, comes to the rescue.

It's a sweet story – though if I ever had a poodle, I'd give him a simple all-over lamb cut.

JๅS

🐾 OSBERT 🐾

It was the day before Aunt Cathy's wedding. Everything glistened and gleamed with excitement. Then the blow fell. Father said: 'We must get some neighbor to take Osbert tomorrow.'

Osbert had been in the family since he was a month old. When first he had come to the house it had been thought that maybe he would develop into some kind of terrier. As he grew, it was discovered he was mostly black poodle whose hair had forgotten to curl. He was as much a part of the family as the children. It was impossible to think of him missing anything that was going on. Peter gasped.

'Goodness, Dad, that's an awfully mean thing to

say even in fun.'

Ann, the eldest, left the breakfast table. She put her arms round Osbert's neck.

'Don't you listen, old man, of course you'll be here for the wedding.'

The face of Andrew, the youngest, was red as a geranium with indignation.

'And you're going to have a great big slice of wedding cake all to yourself.'

The next youngest, Jane, looked severely at her father.

'If anyone but us was listening they might think you meant it.'

Their father hated the children to think him mean, but Osbert was really a very queer-looking dog to attend a smart wedding. He put on his most off-to-the-office-don't-stop-me-now look.

'It's no good arguing. Osbert is to be away all tomorrow. I leave it to you to fix.'

The children went into committee.

'Fancy,' Ann said, 'not inviting him just because he's homely.'

Peter kicked angrily at the table leg.

'A fat lot of guests would be coming to this wedding if everybody who was homely wasn't invited.'

Jane sighed.

'If only he had curly hair like other poodles.'

Ann jumped.

'Fetch your money-boxes.'

Andrew asked: 'What for?'

Ann skipped with pride at her good idea.

'To take Osbert to the hairdresser.'

Monsieur Toto had been doing ladies' hair all day. He was hot, and glad it was time to shut his shop. Then his doorbell clanged. He did not look round to see who had come in.

'I'm closed. If you wish anything, come in another day.'

Peter, as the eldest male, was carrying the money. He laid it down slowly. It was a most impressive sight. The entire savings of four money-boxes for nearly a year. Four dollar bills, two half-dollars, seventeen quarters, thirty-seven dimes, and ten nickels.

Monsieur Toto turned at the clink of money. Ann's words fell over each other.

'All this is for you if you will make Osbert beautiful.'

'Which is Osbert?'

The children did not speak. They pointed. Monsieur Toto gulped. There was a glassy look in his eyes. The children said all together: 'Curls.'

Monsieur Toto was tired. Osbert had a great deal of hair and all of it very straight.

'That is impossible.'

Jane gave a despairing howl. She knelt by Osbert, the tears pouring down her cheeks.

'Darling, darling Osbert, he won't do it. He won't do it.'

Monsieur Toto hated to see a child cry. 'Let me hear exactly why you wish Osbert curled, but, mind you, this is discussion only. I promise nothing.'

It was the wedding morning. The sun shone, men came and arranged flowers and silver bells. The children's mother fussed in and out of the kitchen. Aunt Cathy ran about arranging her wedding presents. Happiness could be felt like a soft wind. Only the children could not enjoy the day. They could think of nothing but twelve o'clock. At twelve o'clock Monsieur Toto had said Osbert might be fetched. It was a difficult job, for at twelve o'clock the girls should be putting on their pink bridesmaids' dresses and the boys their best suits. It had been decided that Peter was the one most easily to be spared. They hoped their mother would be so busy fussing over the girls she might not notice that he was not there.

Their mother did notice, for at one o'clock relations

would arrive.

'Where,' she asked, 'is Peter?'

The children did not answer, so she called their father. He asked, too: 'Where is Peter?'

Ann saw they had to confess.

'He's gone to fetch Osbert.'

Father's voice for once was angry.

'Fetch Osbert! But I said Osbert was to go to a neighbor.'

Ann nodded.

'I know, but we . . . we thought . . .'

There were feet running up the path. Peter opened the front door, but did not himself come in. Instead, in walked a dog who, for a moment, nobody recognized.

Monsieur Toto had done a wonderful job. He had given Osbert a permanent wave. Where once had been lank hair were now little tight curls. He had shampooed him with a very expensive shampoo. He had clipped him. His legs now seemed to be wearing ebony cowboy trousers. His tail had been shaved except for the very tip where there was a bunch of curls. Parts of the rest of him had been clipped, but not his head. On that was a festoon of curls tied with a yellow bow. In the bow was fastened a spray of orange blossom.

The wedding started. When every guest had arrived, a photographer came to take pictures of the wedding group.

The bride and bridegroom.

The groom's father and mother.

The children's father and mother.

Ann and Jane, gorgeous in pink.

Andrew and Peter, curiously tidy and washed. But what held the eyes of all the guests was the center of the group. Sitting in front of the bride and groom and trying not to look self-conscious was Osbert. A paragon of a dog. Glistening, yellow-bowed perfection.

The guests forgot their party manners. They even forgot to say, 'Bless the bride.' Instead, there burst from them a thought they could not hold back.

'Surely that is the most beautiful dog in the world.'

A DOG SO SMALL

by Philippa Pearce

Philippa Pearce has always been revered in the children's book world. I remember reading Tom's Midnight Garden *to my daughter Emma and us both thinking it a perfect book.* A Dog So Small *is almost as good – and a lovely story if you're desperate to have your own dog and can't have one.*

I remember going to a children's literature conference long ago, when I'd only just begun to write children's books. I didn't know many people there, and sat down shyly next to a white-haired lady I thought was perhaps a retired teacher or librarian. She gave me a beaming smile and started chatting away, asking me all sorts of questions and seemingly really interested. It was a full fifteen minutes before I realized she was a writer herself – but it was only when she modestly referred to a recent television adaptation of one of her books, that I realized she was Philippa Pearce!

I was thrilled to have met her and always remember our conversation with affection and gratitude.

JꞶ

🐾 A DOG SO SMALL 🐾

They caught the bus by the skin of their teeth. Ben was carrying Uncle Willy's picture stuffed into his pocket.

In the station at Castleford, the London train was already in, but with some time to wait before it left. Grandpa would not go before that, so Ben leant out of the carriage window to talk to him. There seemed nothing to talk about in such a short time and at a railway station. They found themselves speaking of subjects they would have preferred to leave alone, and saying things that they had not quite intended.

'Tilly didn't know you were off for good this morning,' said Grandpa. 'She'll look for you later today. She'll miss you.'

267

'I'll miss her,' said Ben.

'Pity you can't take her to London for a bit.'

'She'd hate London,' said Ben. 'Nowhere for a dog to go, near us. Even the river's too dirty and dangerous to swim in.'

'Ah!' said Grandpa, and looked at the station clock: minutes to go. 'When you thought we should send you a dog, did you think of the spaniel kind, like her?'

'No,' said Ben. He also looked at the clock. 'As a matter of fact – well, do you know borzois?'

'What! Those tall, thin dogs with long noses and curly hair? *Those*?'

'Only one. Or an Irish wolfhound.'

'A *wolfhound*?'

'Or a mastiff.'

'A—' Grandpa's voice failed him; he looked dazed. 'But they're all such big dogs. And grand, somehow. And . . . and . . .' He tried to elaborate his first idea. 'And – well, you've got to admit it: so *big*.'

'I wasn't exactly expecting one like that. I was just thinking of it.'

'You couldn't keep such a *big* dog – not in London,' Grandpa said.

'I couldn't even keep a small dog.'

'Perhaps, now,' Grandpa said, 'a really *small* dog—'

The porters were slamming the doors at last; the

train was whistling; the guard had taken his green flag from under his arm.

'Not the smallest,' said Ben, and hoped that his grandfather would accept that as final.

'But surely, boy–'

'Not even the smallest dog of the smallest breed.'

'No?'

'Not even a dog so small . . . so small . . .' Ben was frowning, screwing up his eyes, trying to think how he could convince an obstinately hopeful old man. The train was beginning to move. Grandpa was beginning to trot beside it, waiting for Ben to finish his sentence, as though it would be of some help.

'*Not even a dog so small you can only see it with your eyes shut,*' Ben said.

'What?' shouted Grandpa; but it was now too late to talk even in shouts. Ben's absurd remark, the unpremeditated expression of his own despair, went unheard except by Ben himself. The thought, like a letter unposted – unpostable – remained with him.

Ben waved a last goodbye from the window, and then sat down. Something in his pocket knocked against the arm-rest, and he remembered that this must be the picture. He looked up at his suitcase on the rack. It had been difficult enough to get it up there; it would be a nuisance to get it down, just to put the picture inside. Even so, he might have done that, except for the two other people in the compartment; the young man with the illustrated magazines would probably not mind; but there was a much older man reading a sheaf of papers he had brought out of his briefcase. He looked as if he would be against any disturbance, any interruption.

Because he had been thinking of it, Ben quietly took out Uncle Willy's picture and, shielding it with one hand, looked at it. This was the third time he had looked at it.

Still looking at the dog, Chiquitito, he recalled his recent conversation. He could not have the smallest dog of the smallest breed in the world. Not even a dog so small that – if you could imagine such a thing – you could only see it with your eyes shut. No dog.

The feeling of his birthday morning – an absolute misery of disappointed longing – swept over him again. He put the little picture down on the seat behind him, leaned his head back, and closed his eyes, overwhelmed.

He had been staring at the woolwork dog, and now, with his eyes shut, he still saw it, as if it were standing on the carriage-seat opposite. Such visions often appear against shut eyelids, when the open-eyed vision has been particularly intent. Such visions quickly fade; but this did not. The image of the dog remained, exactly as in the picture: a pinky-fawn dog with pointed ears, and pop-eyed.

Only – only the pinky-fawn was not done in wool, and the eye was not a jet bead. This dog was real. First of all, it just stood. Then it stretched itself – first, its forelegs together; then, each hind leg with a separate stretch and shake. Then the dog turned its head to look at Ben, so that Ben saw its other eye and the whole of the other side of its face, which the picture had never shown. But this was not the picture of a dog; it was a real dog – a particular dog.

'Chiquitito,' Ben said; and the dog cocked its head.

THE ACCIDENTAL TOURIST

by Anne Tyler

Children often ask me if I've got a favourite author. I generally reply listing the book I liked the most when I was nine or ten – but the author I most enjoy reading now is Anne Tyler. She writes gentle, quirky family stories about people who are a little odd or obsessive. The Accidental Tourist is probably my favourite out of all her novels. It's got some very funny moments, but it's essentially a sad story – the main character, Macon, has lost his son, and is separated from his wife. He's been left caring for his son's dog, Edward, who's become difficult to handle.

Edward is a wonderful character – and so is Muriel, the woman who manages to tame him.

JW

🐾 THE ACCIDENTAL 🐾 TOURIST

The dog was going with him only as far as the vet's. If he'd known that, he never would have jumped into the car. He sat next to Macon, panting enthusiastically, his keg-shaped body alert with expectation. Macon talked to him in what he hoped was an unalarming tone. 'Hot, isn't it, Edward. You want the air conditioner on?' He adjusted the controls. 'There now. Feeling better?' He heard something unctuous in his voice. Maybe Edward did, too, for he stopped panting and gave Macon a sudden suspicious look. Macon decided to say no more.

They rolled through the neighborhood, down

streets roofed over with trees. They turned into a sunnier section full of stores and service stations. As they neared Murray Avenue, Edward started whimpering. In the parking lot of the Murray Avenue Veterinary Hospital, he somehow became a much smaller animal.

Macon got out of the car and walked around to open the door. When he took hold of Edward's collar, Edward dug his toenails into the upholstery. He had to be dragged all the way to the building, scratching across the hot concrete.

The waiting room was empty. A goldfish tank bubbled in one corner, with a full-colour poster above it illustrating the life cycle of the heartworm. There was a girl on a stool behind the counter, a waifish little person in a halter top.

'I've brought my dog for boarding,' Macon said. He had to raise his voice to be heard above Edward's moans.

Chewing her gum steadily, the girl handed him a printed form and a pencil. 'Ever been here before?' she asked.

'Yes, often.'

'What's the last name?'

'Leary.'

'Leary. Leary,' she said, riffling through a box of

index cards. Macon started filling out the form. Edward was standing upright now and clinging to Macon's knees, like a toddler scared of nursery school.

'Whoa,' the girl said.

She frowned at the card she'd pulled.

'Edward?' she said. 'On Rayford Road?'

'That's right.'

'We can't accept him.'

'What?'

'Says here he bit an attendant. Says, "Bit Barry in the ankle, do not readmit."'

'Nobody told me that.'

'Well, they should have.'

'Nobody said a word! I left him in June when we went to the beach; I came back and they handed him over.'

The girl blinked at him, expressionless.

'Look,' Macon said. 'I'm on my way to the airport, right this minute. I've got a plane to catch.'

'I'm only following orders,' the girl said.

'And what set him off, anyhow?' Macon asked. 'Did anyone think to wonder? Maybe Edward had good reason!'

The girl blinked again. Edward had dropped to all fours by now and was gazing upward with interest, as if following the conversation.

'Ah, the hell with it,' Macon said. 'Come on, Edward.'

He didn't have to take hold of Edward's collar when they left. Edward galloped ahead of him all the way across the parking lot.

In that short time, the car had turned into an oven. Macon opened his window and sat there with the motor idling. What now? He considered going to his sister's, but she probably wouldn't want Edward either. To tell the truth, this wasn't the first time there had been complaints. Last week, for instance, Macon's brother Charles had stopped by to borrow a router, and Edward had darted in a complete circle around his feet, taking furious little nibbles out of his trouser cuffs. Charles was so astonished that he just turned his head slowly, gaping down. 'What's got into him?' he asked. 'He never *used* to do this.' Then when Macon grabbed his collar, Edward had snarled. He'd curled his upper lip and snarled. Could a dog have a nervous breakdown?

Macon wasn't very familiar with dogs. He preferred cats. He liked the way cats kept their own counsel. It was only lately that he'd given Edward any thought at all. Now that he was alone so much he had taken to talking out loud to him, or sometimes he just sat studying him. He admired Edward's intelligent brown eyes and his foxy little face. He appreciated the honey-colored whorls that radiated so symmetrically from the bridge of his nose. And his walk! Ethan used to say that Edward walked as if he had sand in his bathing suit. His rear end waddled busily; his stubby legs seemed hinged by some more primitive mechanism than the legs of taller dogs.

Macon was driving toward home now, for lack of any better idea. He wondered what would happen if he left Edward in the house the way he left the cat, with plenty of food and water. No. Or could Sarah come to see him, two or three times a day? He recoiled from that; it meant asking her. It meant dialing that number he'd never used and asking her for a favor.

MEOW-BOW ANIMAL HOSPITAL, a sign across the street read. Macon braked and Edward lurched forward. 'Sorry,' Macon told him. He made a turn into the parking lot.

The waiting room at the Meow-Bow smelled strongly of disinfectant. Behind the counter stood a thin young woman in a ruffled peasant blouse. She had aggressively frizzy black hair that burgeoned to her shoulders like an Arab headdress. 'Hi, there,' she said to Macon.

Macon said, 'Do you board dogs?'

'Sure.'

'I'd like to board Edward, here.'

She leaned over the counter to look at Edward. Edward panted up at her cheerfully. It was clear he hadn't yet realized what kind of place this was.

'You have a reservation?' the woman asked Macon.

'Reservation! No.'

'Most people reserve.'

'Well, I didn't know that.'

'Especially in the summer.'

'Couldn't you make an exception?'

She thought it over, frowning down at Edward. Her eyes were very small, like caraway seeds, and her face was sharp and colorless.

'Please,' Macon said. 'I'm about to catch a plane. I'm leaving for a week, and I don't have a soul to look after him. I'm desperate, I tell you.'

From the glance she shot at him, he sensed he had surprised her in some way. 'Can't you leave him home with your wife?' she asked.

He wondered how on earth her mind worked.

'If I could do that,' he said, 'why would I be standing here?'

'Oh,' she said. 'You're not married?'

'Well, I am, but she's . . . living elsewhere. They don't allow pets.'

'Oh.'

She came out from behind the counter. She was wearing very short red shorts; her legs were like sticks. 'I'm a divorsy myself,' she said. 'I know what you're going through.'

'And see,' Macon said, 'there's this place I usually board him but they suddenly claim he bites. Claim he bit an attendant and they can't admit him any more.'

'Edward? Do you bite?' the woman said.

Macon realized he should not have mentioned that, but she seemed to take it in stride. 'How could you do such a thing?' she asked Edward. Edward grinned up at her and folded his ears back, inviting a pat. She bent and stroked his head.

'So will you keep him?' Macon said.

'Oh, I guess,' she said, straightening. 'If you're desperate.' She stressed the word – fixing Macon with those small brown eyes – as if giving it more weight than he had intended. 'Fill this out,' she told him, and she handed him a form from a stack on the counter. 'Your name and address and when you'll be back. Don't forget to put when you'll be back.'

Macon nodded, uncapping his fountain pen.

'I'll most likely see you again when you come to pick him up,' she said. 'I mean if you put the time of day to expect you. My name's Muriel.'

'Is this place open evenings?' Macon asked.

'Every evening but Sundays. Till eight.'

'Oh, good.'

'Muriel Pritchett,' she said.

Macon filled out the form while the woman knelt to unbuckle Edward's collar. Edward licked her cheekbone; he must have thought she was just being friendly. So when Macon had finished, he didn't say goodbye. He left the form on the counter and walked out very quickly, keeping a hand in his pocket to silence his keys.

LOVE THAT DOG

by Sharon Creech

Love That Dog *is a hard book to describe. It's a story but it's written as a diary in poetry form. It's a quick, easy read – maybe fifteen minutes? – but it's likely to stay in your mind for a very long time. It's the story of Jack and his beloved rescue dog Sky, and it's a very sad story, but there are funny parts too. I find the reasons why Jack might have to wait ages for the poet Walter Dean Myers to reply to him particularly amusing. They are exactly the same reasons why I can't always reply to every single one of you.*

JᴡS

🐾 LOVE THAT DOG 🐾

My yellow dog
followed me everywhere
every which way I turned
he was there
wagging his tail
and slobber
coming out
of his mouth
when he was smiling
at me
all the time
as if he was
saying

thank you thank you
for choosing me
and jumping up on me
his shaggy straggly paws
on my chest
like he was trying
to hug the insides
right out of me.

And when us kids
were playing outside
kicking the ball
he'd chase after it
and push it with his nose
push push push
and getting slobber
all over the ball
but no one cared
because he was such
a funny dog
that dog Sky
that straggly furry
smiling
dog
Sky.

And I'd call him
every morning
every evening
Hey there, Sky!

THE HUNDRED AND ONE DALMATIANS

by Dodie Smith

You can't get a more gloriously doggy book than The Hundred and One Dalmatians. *I expect you've seen a DVD of the Walt Disney film. I think the book is even better. Dodie Smith wrote it quickly – in seven weeks (my books take me seven months and I'm considered a very prolific author). She didn't need to do any research whatsoever about Dalmatians – she'd adored them for years. Her first Dalmatian was called Pongo, and two others, Buzz and Folly, had a litter of fifteen puppies – in the book Pongo and his Missis have fifteen children too.*

The wondrously evil Cruella de Vil is clearly made up, but apparently Dodie Smith had an actress friend

who took one look at Pongo when he was a puppy and said, 'He would make a nice fur coat.'

If you're a fan of The Hundred and One Dalmatians, do go on to read Dodie Smith's I Capture the Castle. It's a book ideally read in your teens, very different in tone, with no dogs at all – but it's one of my all-time favourite reads.

JwS

❧ THE HUNDRED AND ❧ ONE DALMATIANS

Whilst the dogs searched and the Nannies cried on each other's shoulder, Mrs Dearly telephoned Mr Dearly. He came home at once, bringing with him one of the Top Men from Scotland Yard. The Top Man found a bit of sacking on the area railings and said the puppies must have been dropped into sacks and driven away in the black van. He promised to Comb the Underworld, but warned the Dearlys that stolen dogs were seldom recovered unless a reward was offered. A reward seemed an unreasonable thing to offer a thief, but Mr Dearly was willing to offer it.

He rushed to Fleet Street and had large advertisements put on the front pages of the evening papers (this was rather expensive) and arranged for even larger advertisements to be on the front pages of the next day's morning papers (this was even more expensive). Beyond this, there seemed nothing he or Mrs Dearly could do except try to comfort each other and comfort the Nannies and the dogs. Soon the Nannies stopped crying and joined in the comforting, and prepared beautiful meals which nobody felt like eating. And at last, night fell on the stricken household.

Worn out, the three dogs lay in their baskets in front of the kitchen fire.

'Think of my baby Cadpig in a sack,' said Missis, with a sob.

'Her big brother, Patch, will take care of her,' said Pongo, soothingly – though he felt most unsoothed himself.

'Lucky is so brave, he will bite the thieves,' wailed Perdita. 'And then they will kill him.'

'No, they won't,' said Pongo. 'The pups were stolen because they are valuable. No one will kill them. They are only valuable while they are alive.'

But even as he said this, a terrible suspicion was forming in his mind. And it grew and grew as the night wore on. Long after Missis and Perdita, utterly exhausted, had fallen asleep, he lay awake staring at the fire, chewing the wicker of his basket as a man might have smoked a pipe.

Anyone who did not know Pongo well would have thought him handsome, amusing and charming, but not particularly clever. Even the Dearlys did not quite realise the depths of his mind. He was often still so puppyish. He would run after balls and sticks, climb into laps far too small to hold him, roll over on his back to have his stomach scratched. How was anyone to guess that this playful creature owned one of the keenest brains in Dogdom?

It was at work now. All through the long December night he put two and two together and made four. Once or twice he almost made five.

He had no intention of alarming Missis or Perdita with his suspicions. Poor Pongo! He not only suffered on his own account, as a father; he also suffered on the account of two mothers. (For he had come to feel the puppies had two mothers, though he never felt he had two wives – he looked on Perdita as a much-loved young sister.) He would say nothing about his worst fears until he was quite sure. Meanwhile, there was an important task ahead of him. He was still planning it when the Nannies came down to start another day.

As a rule, this was a splendid time – with the fire freshly made, plenty of food around and the puppies at their most playful. This morning – well, as Nanny Butler said, it just didn't bear thinking about. But she thought about it, and so did everybody else in that pup-less house.

No good news came during the day, but the Dearlys were surprised and relieved to find that the dogs ate well. (Pongo had been firm: 'You girls have got to keep your strength up.') And there was an even greater surprise in the afternoon. Pongo and Missis showed very plainly that they wanted to take the Dearlys for a walk. Perdita did not. She was determined to stay at home in case any pup returned and was in need of a wash.

Cold weather had come at last – Christmas was only a week away.

'Missis must wear her coat,' said Mrs Dearly.

It was a beautiful blue coat with a white binding; Missis was very proud of it. Coats had been bought for Pongo and Perdita, too. But Pongo had made it clear he disliked wearing his.

So the coat was put on Missis, and both dogs were dressed in their handsome chain collars. And then they put the Dearlys on their leashes and led them into the park.

From the first, it was clear the dogs knew just where they wanted to go. Very firmly, they led the way right across the park, across the road, and to the open space which is called Primrose Hill. This did not surprise the Dearlys as it had always been a favourite walk. What did surprise them was the way Pongo and Missis behaved when they got to the top of the hill. They stood side by side and they barked.

They barked to the north, they barked to the south, they barked to the east and west. And each time they changed their positions, they began the barking with three very strange, short, sharp barks.

'Anyone would think they were signalling,' said Mr Dearly.

But he did not really mean it. And they *were* signalling.

Many people must have noticed how dogs like to bark in the early evening. Indeed, twilight has sometimes been called 'Dogs' Barking Time'. Busy town dogs bark less than country dogs, but all dogs know all about the Twilight Barking. It is their way of keeping in touch with distant friends, passing on important news, enjoying a good gossip. But none of the dogs who answered Pongo and Missis expected to enjoy a gossip, for the three short, sharp barks meant: 'Help! Help! Help!'

No dog sends that signal unless the need is desperate. And no dog who hears it ever fails to respond.

Within a few minutes, the news of the stolen puppies was travelling across England, and every dog who heard at once turned detective. Dogs living in London's Underworld (hard-bitten characters; also hard-biting) set out to explore sinister alleys where dog thieves lurk. Dogs in Pet Shops hastened to make quite sure all puppies offered for sale were not Dalmatians in disguise. And dogs who could do nothing else swiftly handed on the news, spreading it through London and on through the suburbs, and on, on to the open country: 'Help! Help! Help! Fifteen Dalmatian puppies stolen. Send news to Pongo and Missis Pongo, of Regent's Park, London. End of Message.'

Pongo and Missis hoped all this would be happening. But all they really knew was that they had made contact with the dogs near enough to answer them, and that these dogs would be standing by, at twilight the next evening, to relay any news that had come along.

One Great Dane, over towards Hampstead, was particularly encouraging.

'I have a chain of friends all over England,' he said, in his great, booming bark. 'And I will be on duty day and night. Courage, courage, O Dogs of Regent's Park!'

It was almost dark now. And the Dearlys were suggesting – very gently – that they should be taken home. So after a few last words, 'What about coming home, boy?' For the first time in his life, Pongo jerked his head from Mr Dearly's hand, then went on standing stock still. And at last the Great Dane spoke again, booming triumphantly through the gathering dusk.

'Calling Pongo and Missis Pongo. News! News at last! Stand by to receive details.'

A most wonderful thing had happened. Just as the Great Dane had been about to sign off, a Pomeranian with a piercing yap had got through to him. She had heard it from a Poodle who had heard it from a Boxer who had heard it from a Pekinese. Dogs of almost every known breed had helped to carry the news – and a great many dogs of unknown breed (none the worse for that and all of them bright as buttons). In all, four hundred and eighty dogs had relayed the message, which had travelled over sixty miles as the dog barks. Each dog had given the 'Urgent' signal, which had silenced all gossiping dogs. Not that many dogs were merely gossiping that night; almost all the Twilight Barking had been about the missing puppies.

This was the strange story that now came through

to Pongo and Missis: some hours earlier, an elderly English Sheepdog, living on a farm in a remote Suffolk village, had gone for an afternoon amble. He knew all about the missing puppies and had just been discussing them with the tabby cat at the farm. She was a great friend of his.

Some little way from the village, on a lonely heath, was an old house completely surrounded by an unusually high wall. Two brothers named Saul and Jasper Baddun lived there, but were merely caretakers for the real owner. The place had an evil reputation – no local dog would have dreamed of putting its nose inside the tall iron gates. In any case, these gates were always kept locked.

It so happened that the Sheepdog's walk took him past this house. He quickened his pace, having no wish to meet either of the Badduns. And at that moment, something came sailing out over the high wall.

It was a bone, the Sheepdog saw with pleasure; but not a bone with meat on it, he noted with disgust. It was an old, dry bone, and on it were some peculiar scratches. The scratches formed letters. And the letters were S.O.S.

Someone was asking for help! Someone behind the tall wall and the high, chained gates! The Sheepdog barked a low, curious bark. He was answered by a high, shrill bark. Then he heard a yelp, as if some dog had been cuffed. The Sheepdog barked again, saying: 'I'll do all I can.' Then he picked up the bone in his teeth and raced back to the farm.

Once home, he showed the bone to the tabby cat and asked her help. Then, together, they hurried to the lonely house. At the back, they found a tree whose branches reached over the wall. The cat climbed the tree, went along its branches, and then leapt to a tree the other side of the wall.

'Take care of yourself,' barked the Sheepdog. 'Remember those Baddun brothers are villains.'

The cat clawed her way down, backwards, to the ground, then hurried through the overgrown shrubbery. Soon she came to an old brick wall which enclosed a stable-yard. From behind the wall came whimperings and snufflings. She leapt to the top of the wall and looked down.

The next second, one of the Baddun brothers saw her and threw a stone at her. She dodged it, jumped from the wall and ran for her life. In two minutes she was safely back with the Sheepdog.

'They're there!' she said triumphantly. 'The place is *seething* with Dalmatian puppies!'

The Sheepdog was a formidable Twilight Barker.

Tonight, with the most important news in Dogdom to send out, he surpassed himself. And so the message travelled, by way of farm dogs and house dogs, great dogs and small dogs. Sometimes a bark would carry half a mile or more, sometimes it would only need to carry a few yards. One sharp-eared Cairn saved the chain from breaking by picking up a bark from nearly a mile away, and then almost bursting herself getting it on to the dog next door. Across miles and miles of country, across miles and miles of suburbs, across a network of London streets the chain held firm; from the depths of Suffolk to the top of Primrose Hill – where Pongo and Missis, still as statues, stood listening, listening.

'Puppies found in lonely house. S.O.S. on old bone–' Missis could not take it all in. But Pongo missed nothing. There were instructions on reaching the village, suggestions for the journey, offers of hospitality on the way. And the dog chain was standing by to take a message back to the pups – the Sheepdog would bark it over the wall in the dead of night.

At first Missis was too excited to think of anything to say, but Pongo barked clearly: 'Tell them we're coming! Tell them we start tonight! Tell them to be brave!'

Then Missis found her voice: 'Give them all our

love! Tell Patch to take care of Cadpig! Tell Lucky not to be too daring! Tell Roly Poly to keep out of mischief!' She would have sent a message to every one of the fifteen pups if Pongo had not whispered: 'That's enough, dear. We mustn't make it too complicated. Let the Great Dane start work now.'

So they signed off and there was a sudden silence. And then, though not quite so loudly, they heard the Great Dane again. But this time he was not barking towards them. What they heard was their message, starting on its way to Suffolk.

JUST WILLIAM

by Richmal Crompton

I've always loved reading aloud. When my daughter Emma could easily read for herself, we still carried on our special reading-aloud sessions, working our way through many wonderful children's classics. The William books were always a great success. They're a joy to read aloud because they're so funny – William's speeches are all fantastic. I pride myself on my eleven-year-old boy impersonation!

The following chapter is the memorable story of how William acquires his dog Jumble – an animal with almost as much personality as his owner.

J.W.

❧ JUST WILLIAM ❧

Jumble

William's father carefully placed the bow and arrow at the back of the library cupboard, then closed the cupboard door and locked it in grim silence. William's eyes, large, reproachful, and gloomy, followed every movement.

'Three windows and Mrs Clive's cat all in one morning,' began Mr Brown sternly.

'I didn't *mean* to hit that cat,' said William earnestly. 'I didn't – honest. I wouldn't go round teasin' cats. They get so mad at you, cats do. It jus' got in the way. I couldn't stop shootin' in time. An' I didn't *mean* to break those windows. I wasn't *tryin'* to hit them. I've not hit anything I was trying to hit yet,' he said wistfully. 'I've not got into it. It's jus' a knack. It jus' wants practice.'

Mr Brown pocketed the key.

'It's a knack you aren't likely to acquire by practice on this instrument,' he said drily.

William wandered out into the garden and looked sadly up at the garden wall. But the Little Girl Next Door was away and could offer no sympathy, even if he climbed up to his precarious seat on the top. Fate was against him in every way. With a deep sigh he went out of the garden gate and strolled down the road disconsolately, hands in pockets.

Life stretched empty and uninviting before him without his bow and arrow. And Ginger would have his bow and arrow, Henry would have his bow and arrow, Douglas would have his bow and arrow. He, William, alone would be a thing apart, a social outcast, a boy without a bow and arrow; for bows and arrows were the fashion. If only one of the others would break a window or hit a silly old cat that hadn't the sense to keep out of the way.

He came to a stile leading into a field and took his seat upon it dejectedly, his elbows on his knees, his chin in his hands. Life was simply not worth living.

'A rotten old cat!' he said aloud. 'A rotten old cat! – and didn't even hurt it! – it made a fuss – jus' out of spite, screamin' and carryin' on! And windows – as if glass wasn't cheap enough – and easy to put in! I could – I could mend 'em myself – if I'd got the stuff to do it. I—' He stopped. Something was coming down the road. It came jauntily with a light, dancing step, fox-terrier ears cocked, retriever-nose raised, collie-tail wagging, slight dachshund body aquiver with the joy of life.

It stopped in front of William with a glad bark of welcome, then stood eager, alert, friendly, a mongrel unashamed.

'Rats! Fetch 'em out!' said William idly.

It gave a little spring and waited, front paws apart and crouching, a waggish eye upraised to William. William broke off a stick from the hedge and threw it. His visitor darted after it with a shrill bark, took it up, worried it, threw it into the air, caught it, growled at it, finally brought it back to William and panting, eager, unmistakably grinning, begging for more.

William's drooping spirits revived. He descended from his perch and examined its collar. It bore the one word 'Jumble'.

'Hey! Jumble!' he called, setting off down the road.

Jumble jumped up around him, dashed off, dashed back, worried his boots, jumped up at him again in wild, eager friendship, dashed off again, begged for another stick, caught it, rolled over with it, growled at it, then chewed it up and laid the remains at William's feet.

'Good ole chap!' said William encouragingly. 'Good ole Jumble! Come on, then.'

Jumble came on. William walked through the village with a self-conscious air of proud yet careless ownership, while Jumble gambolled round his heels.

Every now and then he would turn his head and whistle imperiously, to recall his straying protégé from the investigation of ditches and roadside. It was a whistle, commanding, controlling, yet withal careless, that William had sometimes practised privately in readiness for the blissful day when Fate should present him with a real live dog of his own. So far Fate, in the persons of his father and mother, had been proof against all his pleading.

William passed a blissful morning. Jumble swam in the pond, he fetched sticks out of it, he shook himself violently all over William, he ran after a hen, he was chased by a cat, he barked at a herd of cows, he pulled down a curtain that was hanging out in a cottage garden to dry – he was mischievous, affectionate, humorous, utterly irresistible – and he completely adopted William. William would turn a corner with a careless swagger and then watch breathlessly to see if the rollicking, frisky little figure would follow, and always it came tearing eagerly after him.

William was rather late to lunch. His father and mother and elder brother and sister were just beginning the meal. He slipped quietly and unostentatiously into his seat. His father was reading a newspaper. Mr Brown always took two daily papers, one of which he perused at breakfast and the other at lunch.

'William,' said Mrs Brown, 'I do wish you'd be on time, and I do wish you'd brush your hair before you come to table.'

William raised a hand to perform the operation, but catching sight of its colour, hastily lowered it.

'No, Ethel dear, I didn't know anyone had taken Lavender Cottage. An artist? How nice! William dear, *do* sit still. Have they moved in yet?'

'Yes,' said Ethel, 'they've taken it furnished for two months, I think. Oh, my goodness, just *look* at William's hands!'

William put his hands under the table and glared at her.

'Go and wash your hands, dear,' said Mrs Brown patiently.

For eleven years she had filled the trying position of William's mother. It had taught her patience.

William rose reluctantly.

'They're not dirty,' he said in a tone of righteous indignation. 'Well, anyway, they've been dirtier other times and you've said nothin'. I can't *always* be washin' them, can I? Some sorts of hands get dirty quicker than others an' if you keep on washin' it only makes them worse an'—'

Ethel groaned and William's father lowered his paper. William withdrew quickly but with an air of dignity.

'And just *look* at his boots!' said Ethel as he went. 'Simply caked; and his stockings are soaking wet – you can see from here. He's been right *in* the pond by the look of him and—'

William heard no more. There were moments when he actively disliked Ethel.

He returned a few minutes later, shining with cleanliness, his hair brushed back fiercely off his face.

'His *nails*,' murmured Ethel as he sat down.

'Well,' said Mrs Brown, 'go on telling us about the new people. William, do hold your knife properly, dear. Yes, Ethel?'

William finished his meal in silence, then brought

forth his momentous announcement.

'I've gotter dog,' he said with an air of importance.

'What sort of dog?' and 'Who gave it to you?' said Robert and Ethel simultaneously.

'No one gave it me,' he said. 'I jus' got it. It began following me this morning, an' I couldn't get rid of it. It wouldn't go, anyway. It followed me all round the village an' it came home with me. I couldn't get rid of it, anyhow.'

'Where is it now?' said Mrs Brown anxiously.

'In the back garden.'

Mr Brown folded up his paper.

'Digging up my flower beds, I suppose,' he said with despairing resignation.

'He's tied up all right,' William assured him. 'I tied him to the tree in the middle of the rose bed.'

'The rose bed!' groaned his father. 'Good Lord!'

'Has he had anything to eat?' demanded Robert sternly.

'Yes,' said William, avoiding his mother's eye. 'I found a few bits of old things for him in the larder.'

William's father took out his watch and rose from the table.

'Well, you'd better take it to the Police Station this afternoon,' he said shortly.

'The Police Station!' repeated William hoarsely. 'It's not a *lost* dog. It – it jus' doesn't belong to anyone, at least it didn't. Poor thing,' he said feelingly. 'It – it doesn't want *much* to make it happy. It can sleep in my room an' jus' eat scraps.'

Mr Brown went out without answering.

'You'll have to take it, you know, William,' said Mrs Brown, 'so be quick. You know where the Police Station is, don't you? Shall I come with you?'

'No, thank you,' said William hastily.

A few minutes later he was walking down to the Police Station followed by the still eager Jumble, who trotted along, unconscious of his doom.

Upon William's face was a set, stern expression which cleared slightly as he neared the Police Station. He stood at the gate and looked at Jumble. Jumble placed his front paws ready for a game and wagged his tail.

'Well,' said William, 'here you are. Here's the Police Station.'

Jumble gave a shrill bark. 'Hurry up with that stick or that race, whichever you like,' he seemed to say.

'Well, go in,' said William, nodding his head in the direction of the door.

Jumble began to worry a big stone in the road. He rolled it along with his paws, then ran after it with fierce growls.

'Well, it's the Police Station,' said William. 'Go in if you want.'

With that he turned on his heel and walked home, without one backward glance. But he walked slowly, with many encouraging 'Hey! Jumbles' and many short commanding whistles. And Jumble trotted happily at his heels. There was no one in the garden, there was no one in the hall, there was no one on the stairs. Fate was for once on William's side.

William appeared at the tea table well washed and brushed, wearing that air of ostentatious virtue that those who knew him best connected with his most daring coups.

'Did you take that dog to the Police Station, William?' said William's father.

William coughed.

'Yes, Father,' he said meekly with his eyes upon his plate.

'What did they say about it?'

'Nothing, Father.'

'I suppose I'd better spend the evening replanting those rose trees,' went on his father bitterly.

'And William gave him a *whole* steak and kidney pie,' murmured Mrs Brown. 'Cook will have to make another for tomorrow.'

William coughed again politely, but did not raise his eyes from his plate.

'What is that noise?' said Ethel. 'Listen!'

They sat, listening intently. There was a dull grating sound as of the scratching of wood.

'It's upstairs,' said Robert with the air of a Sherlock Holmes.

Then came a shrill, impatient bark.

'It's a *dog*!' said the four of them simultaneously. 'It's William's dog.'

They all turned horrified eyes upon William, who coloured slightly but continued to eat a piece of cake with an unconvincing air of abstraction.

'I thought you said you'd taken that dog to the Police Station, William,' said Mr Brown sternly.

'I did,' said William with decision. 'I did take it to the Police Station an' I came home. I s'pose it must of got out an' come home an' gone up into my bedroom.'

'Where did you leave it? In the Police Station?'

'No – at it – jus' at the gate.'

Mr Brown rose with an air of weariness.

'Robert,' he said, 'will you please see that that animal goes to the Police Station this evening?'

'Yes, Father,' said Robert, with a vindictive glare at William.

William followed him upstairs.

'Beastly nuisance!' muttered Robert.

Jumble, who was chewing William's door, greeted them ecstatically.

'Look!' said William bitterly. 'Look at how it knows one! Nice thing to send a dog that knows one like that to the Police Station! Mean sort of trick!'

Robert surveyed it coldly.

'Rotten little mongrel!' he said from the heights of superior knowledge.

'Mongrel!' said William indignantly. 'There jus' isn't no mongrel about *him*. Look at him! An' he can learn tricks easy as easy. Look at him sit up and beg. I only taught him this afternoon.'

He took a biscuit out of his pocket and held it up. Jumble rose unsteadily on to his hind legs and tumbled over backwards. He wagged his tail and grinned, intensely amused. Robert's expression of superiority relaxed.

'Do it again,' he said. 'Not so far back. Here! Give it me. Come on, come on, old chap! That's it! Now stay there! Stay there! Good dog! Got any more? Let's try him again.'

During the next twenty minutes they taught him

to sit up and almost taught him 'Trust' and 'Paid for'. There was certainly a charm about Jumble. Even Robert felt it. Then Ethel's voice came up the stairs.

'Robert! Sydney Bellew's come for you.'

'Blow the wretched dog!' said the fickle Robert, rising, red and dishevelled from stooping over Jumble. 'We were going to walk to Fairfields and the beastly Police Station's right out of our way.'

'I'll take it, Robert,' said William kindly. 'I will really.'

Robert eyed him suspiciously.

'Yes, you took it this afternoon, didn't you?'

'I will, honest, tonight, Robert. Well, I couldn't, could I – after all this?'

'I don't know,' said Robert darkly. 'No one ever knows what *you* are going to do!'

Sydney's voice came up.

'Hurry up, old chap! We shall never have time to do it before dark, if you aren't quick.'

'I'll take him, honest, Robert.'

Robert hesitated and was lost.

'Well,' he said, 'you just mind you do, that's all, or I'll jolly well hear about it. I'll see *you* do too.'

So William started off once more towards the Police Station with Jumble, still blissfully happy, at his heels. William walked slowly, eyes fixed on the ground, brows knit in deep thought. It was very rarely that William admitted himself beaten.

'Hello, William!'

William looked up.

Ginger stood before him holding his bow and arrows ostentatiously.

'You've had your bow and arrow took off you!' he jeered.

William fixed his eyes moodily upon him for a minute, then very gradually his eyes brightened and his face cleared. William had an idea.

'If I give you a dog half time,' he said slowly, 'will you give me your bow and arrows half time?'

'Where's your dog?' said Ginger suspiciously.

William did not turn his head.

'There's one behind me, isn't there?' he said anxiously. 'Hey, Jumble!'

'Oh, yes, he's just come out of the ditch.'

'Well,' continued William, 'I'm taking him to the Police Station and I'm just goin' on an' he's following me and if you take him off me I won't see you 'cause I won't turn round and jus' take hold of his collar an' he's called Jumble an' take him up to the old barn and we'll keep him there an' join at him and feed him days and days about and you let me practise on your bow and arrow. That's fair, isn't it?'

Ginger considered thoughtfully.

'All right,' he said laconically.

William walked on to the Police Station without turning round.

'Well?' whispered Robert sternly that evening.

'I took him, Robert – least – I started off with him, but when I'd got there he'd gone. I looked round and he'd jus' gone. I couldn't see him anywhere, so I came home.'

'Well, if he comes to this house again,' said Robert, 'I'll wring his neck, so just you look out.'

Two days later William sat in the barn on an upturned box, chin in hands, gazing down at Jumble. A paper bag containing Jumble's ration for the day lay beside him. It was his day of ownership. The collecting of Jumble's 'scraps' was a matter of infinite care and trouble. They consisted of – a piece of bread that William had managed to slip into his pocket during breakfast, a piece of meat he had managed to slip into his pocket during dinner, a jam puff stolen from the larder and a bone removed from the dustbin. Ginger roamed the fields with his bow and arrow while William revelled in the ownership of Jumble. Tomorrow William would roam the fields with bow and arrow and Ginger would assume ownership of Jumble.

William had spent the morning teaching Jumble

several complicated tricks, and adoring him more and more completely each moment. He grudged him bitterly to Ginger, but – the charm of the bow and arrow was strong. He wished to terminate the partnership, to resign Ginger's bow and arrow and take the irresistible Jumble wholly to himself. He thought of the bow and arrow in the library cupboard; he thought, planned, plotted, but could find no way out. He did not see a man come to the door of the barn and stand there leaning against the doorpost watching him. He was a tall man with a thin, lean face and a loose-fitting tweed suit. As his eyes lit upon William and Jumble they narrowed suddenly and his mobile lips curved into a slight, unconscious smile. Jumble saw him first and went towards him wagging his tail. William looked up and scowled ungraciously. The stranger raised his hat.

'Good afternoon,' he said politely. 'Do you remember what you were thinking about just then?'

William looked at him with a certain interest, speculating upon his probable insanity. He imagined lunatics were amusing people.

'Yes.'

'Well, if you'll think of it again and look just like that, I'll give you anything you like. It's a rash promise, but I will.'

William promptly complied. He quite forgot the presence of the strange man, who took a little block out of his pocket and began to sketch William's inscrutable, brooding face.

'Daddy!'

The man sighed and put away his block.

'You'll do it again for me one day, won't you, and I'll keep my promise? Hello!'

A little girl appeared now at the barn door, dainty, dark-eyed and exquisitely dressed. She threw a lightning flash at the occupants of the barn.

'Daddy!' she screamed. 'It's Jumble! It *is* Jumble! Oh, you horrid dog-stealing boy!'

Jumble ran to her with shrill barks of welcome, then ran back to William to reassure him of his undying loyalty.

'It *is* Jumble,' said the man. 'He's called Jumble,' he explained to William, 'because he is a jumble. He's all sorts of a dog, you know. This is Ninette, my daughter, and my name is Jarrow, and we've taken Lavender Cottage for two months. We're roving vagabonds. We never stay anywhere longer than two months. So now you know all about us. Jumble seems to have adopted you. Ninette, my dear, you are completely ousted from Jumble's heart. This gentleman reigns supreme.'

'I *didn't* steal him,' said William indignantly. 'He

just came. He began following me. I didn't want him to – not jus' at first anyway, not much anyway. I suppose,' a dreadful fear came to his heart, 'I suppose you want him back?'

'You can keep him for a bit if you want him, can't he, Daddy? Daddy's going to buy me a Pom – a dear little white Pom. When we lost Jumble, I thought I'd rather have a Pom. Jumble's so rough and he's not really a *good* dog. I mean he's no pedigree.'

'Then I can keep him jus' for a bit?' said William, his voice husky with eagerness.

'Oh, yes. I'd much rather have a quieter sort of dog. Would you like to come and see our cottage? It's just over here.'

William, slightly bewildered but greatly relieved, set off with her. Mr Jarrow followed slowly behind. It appeared that Miss Ninette Jarrow was rather a wonderful person. She was eleven years old. She had visited every capital in Europe, seen the best art and heard the best music in each. She had been to every play then on in London. She knew all the newest dances.

'Do you like Paris?' she asked William as they went towards Lavender Cottage.

'Never been there,' said William stolidly, glancing round surreptitiously to see that Jumble was following.

She shook her dark curly head from side to side – a little trick she had.

'You funny boy. *Mais vous parlez français, n'est ce pas?'*

William disdained to answer. He whistled to Jumble, who was chasing an imaginary rabbit in a ditch.

'Can you jazz?' she asked.

'I don't know,' he said guardedly. 'I've not tried. I expect I could.'

She took a few flying graceful steps with slim black silk-encased legs.

'That's it. I'll teach you at home. We'll dance it to a gramophone.'

William walked on in silence.

She stopped suddenly under a tree and held up her little vivacious, piquant face to him.

'You can kiss me if you like,' she said.

William looked at her dispassionately.

'I don't want to, thanks,' he said politely.

'Oh, you *are* a funny boy!' she said with a ripple of laughter. 'And you look so rough and untidy. You're rather like Jumble. Do you like Jumble?'

'Yes,' said William. His voice had a sudden quaver in it. His ownership of Jumble was a thing of the past.

'You can have him for always and always,' she said suddenly. '*Now* kiss me!'

He kissed her cheek awkwardly with an air of one determined to do his duty, but with a great, glad relief at his heart.

'I'd love to see you dance,' she laughed. 'You *would* look funny.'

She took a few more fairy steps.

'You've seen Pavlova, haven't you?'

'Dunno.'

'You must know.'

'I mustn't,' said William, irritably. 'I might have seen him and not known it was him, mightn't I?'

She raced back to her father with another ripple of laughter.

'He's *such* a funny boy, Daddy, and he can't jazz and he's never seen Pavlova, and he can't talk French and I've given him Jumble and he didn't want to kiss me!'

Mr Jarrow fixed William with a drily quizzical smile.

'Beware, young man,' he said. 'She'll try to educate you. I know her. I warn you.'

As they got to the door of Lavender Cottage he turned to William.

'Now just sit and think for a minute. I'll keep my promise.'

'I do like you,' said Ninette graciously as he took his departure. 'You must come again. I'll teach you heaps of things. I think I'd like to marry you when we grow up. You're so – *restful.*'

William came home the next afternoon to find Mr Jarrow in the armchair in the library talking to his father.

'I was just dry for a subject,' he was saying; 'at my wits' end, and when I saw them there, I had a heaven-sent inspiration. Ah! Here he is. Ninette wants you to come to tea tomorrow, William. Ninette's given him Jumble. Do you mind?' he said, turning to Mr Brown.

Mr Brown swallowed hard.

'I'm trying not to,' he said. 'He kept us all awake last night, but I suppose we'll get used to it.'

'And I made him a rash promise,' went on Mr Jarrow, 'and I'm jolly well going to keep it if it's humanly possible. William, what would you like best in all the world?'

William fixed his eyes unflinchingly upon his father.

'I'd like my bow and arrows back out of that cupboard,' he said firmly.

Mr Jarrow looked at William's father beseechingly.

'Don't let me down,' he implored. 'I'll pay for all the damage.'

Slowly and with a deep sigh Mr Brown drew a bunch of keys from his pocket.

'It means that we all go once more in hourly peril of our lives,' he said resignedly.

After tea William set off again down the road. The setting sun had turned the sky to gold. There was a soft haze over all the countryside. The clear birdsongs filled all the air, and the hedgerows were bursting into summer. And through it all marched William, with a slight swagger, his bow under one arm, his arrows under the other, while at his heels trotted Jumble, eager, playful, adoring – a mongrel unashamed – all sorts of a dog. And at William's heart was a proud, radiant happiness.

There was a picture in that year's Academy that attracted a good deal of attention. It was of a boy sitting on an upturned box in a barn, his elbows on his knees, his chin in his hands. He was gazing down at a mongrel dog and in his freckled face was the solemnity and unconscious, eager wistfulness that is the mark of youth. His untidy, unbrushed hair stood up round his face. The mongrel was looking up, some reflection of the boy's eager wistfulness showing in the eyes and cocked ears. It was called 'Friendship'.

Mrs Brown went to see it. She said it wasn't really a very good likeness of William and she wished they'd made him look a little tidier.

BORN TO RUN

by Michael Morpurgo

There's a picture-book village green not too far from where I live. It has a duck pond, a little white church, a row of cottages with wonderful flower gardens, and a farm shop where I go to buy all my summer fruit and vegetables. One day we were driving past this green when I saw a greyhound – then another and another and another! We had to stop the car to appreciate the amazing sight of at least fifty greyhounds, all with their owners, happily gathering together.

It turned out that this was a special Rescued Greyhound Club. All the proud owners and their dogs meet up every couple of months and go for a lovely long walk in the nearby woods to celebrate their new lives together.

I wondered about writing a story about this – but the King of Animal Stories, Michael Morpurgo, has

written a greyhound novel that can't be surpassed. Born to Run *is a riveting read, subtly dealing with various serious issues. It's a total page-turner. The extract that follows is near the beginning, when Patrick has rescued a sack of greyhound puppies from the canal, and is desperate to keep just one for himself.*

JᴡS

🐾 BORN TO RUN 🐾

All that really mattered now was taking Best Mate home with him and looking after him. His mum kept hugging and kissing him. Patrick wasn't so keen on that, not with everyone else there. So in the end he turned and walked away. He was tired of all the talk, all the chatter going on around him. He wanted to be alone with Best Mate.

But they wouldn't leave him alone. Within a couple of minutes he found there was someone else crouching down beside him. He had on a blue uni-form and a peaked cap. He explained he was from the RSPCA. He spoke with a very soft understanding voice, the kind people use when they know you're not going to like what they're about to say – a bad news voice. He had come to take the puppies away, he told Patrick, and look after them for him. 'We'll find good homes for them all, Patrick. OK?' he said.

'I've got a good home,' Patrick replied. 'So I can keep one of them, can't I?' He looked up at his dad. 'We can, can't we, Dad?' But his dad wasn't saying yes and he wasn't saying no. He was looking down at the floor and saying nothing. His mum was biting her lip. She wouldn't look at him either. That was the moment Patrick realised for the first time that they might not let him take Best Mate home with him.

His dad was crouching down beside him now, his arm around him. 'Patrick,' he said, 'we've talked about this before, about having a dog, haven't we? Remember what we said? We can't keep a dog in the flat. Mum's out at work most of the day. You know she is, and so am I. It wouldn't be fair on him. That's why we got Swimsy instead, remember? You did such a brave and good thing, Patrick. Mum and me, we're so proud of you. But keeping one of these pups just isn't on. You know that. He needs space to play, room to run in.'

'We've got the park, Dad,' Patrick pleaded, his eyes filling with tears now. 'Please, Dad. Please.' He knew it was hopeless, but he still wouldn't give up.

In the end it was Mrs Brightwell who persuaded him, and that was only because he couldn't argue with her. No one argued with Mrs Brightwell. 'Tell me something, Patrick,' she said, and she was talking to him very gently, very quietly, not in her usual voice at all. 'You didn't save those puppies just so you could have one, did you?'

'No,' he replied.

'No, of course you didn't,' she went on. 'You're not like that. You saved them because they were crying out for help. You gave them their lives back, and that was a truly wonderful thing to do. But now you have to let them go. They'll be well looked after, I promise you.'

Patrick ran out then, unable to stop himself sobbing. He went to the toilet, where he always went when he needed to cry in private. When he got back, the box and the puppies had gone, and so had the man in the peaked cap from the RSPCA.

Mrs Brightwell told Patrick he could have the rest of the day off school, so that was something. His mum and dad took him home in the car. No one spoke a word all the way. He tried to hate them, but he couldn't. He didn't feel angry, he didn't even feel sad. It was as if all his feelings had drained out of him. He didn't cry again. He lay there all day long on his bed, face to the wall. He didn't eat because he wasn't hungry. His mum came in and tried to cheer him up. 'One day,' she told him, 'one day, we'll live in a house with a proper garden. Then we can have a dog. Promise.'

'But it won't be Best Mate, will it?' he said.

A little later his dad came in and sat on his bed. He tried something different. 'After what you did,' he said, 'I reckon you deserve a proper treat. We'll go to the football tomorrow. Local Derby. We'll have a pizza first, margherita, your favourite. What d'you say?'

Patrick said nothing. 'A good night's sleep is what you need,' his dad went on. 'You'll feel a lot better tomorrow. Promise.' Everyone, Patrick thought, was doing an awful lot of promising, and that was always a bad sign.

From up in his room Patrick heard them all evening whispering urgently in the kitchen below – it was loud enough for him to hear almost every word they said. His mum was going on about how she wished they didn't have to live in a flat. 'Never mind a dog,' she was saying, 'Patrick needs a place where he can play out. All kids do. We've been cooped up in this flat all his life.'

'It's a nice flat,' said his dad. 'I like it here.'

'Oh, well then, that's fine, I suppose. Let's stay here for ever, shall we?'

'I didn't mean it like that, you know I didn't.'

It wasn't a proper row, not even a heated argument. There were no raised voices, but they talked of nothing else all evening.

In the end Patrick bored of it, and anyway he was tired. He kept closing his eyes, and whenever he did he found himself living the day through again, the best of it and the worst of it. It was so easy to let his mind roam, simply to drift away of its own accord. He liked where it was taking him. He could see Best Mate, now a fully grown greyhound, streaking across the park, and he could see himself haring after him, then both of them lying there in the grass, the sun blazing down, with Best Mate stretched out beside him, his paw on his arm and gazing lovingly at him out of his wide brown eyes. Patrick fell asleep dreaming of that moment, of Best Mate looking up at him, and even when he woke up he found himself dreaming exactly the same thing. And that was strange, Patrick thought, very strange indeed.

Best Mate was still lying there beside him, only somehow he looked much smaller than he had before, and they weren't outside in the park in the sunshine, and his nose was cold and wet. Patrick knew that because Best Mate was suddenly snuffling at Patrick's ear, licking it, then crawling on top of him and licking his nose as well. That was when he first dared to hope that this was all just too life-like to be a dream, that it might be real, really real. He looked up. His mum and dad were standing there grinning down at him like a couple of cats that had got the cream. The radio was on down in the kitchen, the kettle was whistling and the toast was burning. He was awake. This was happening! It was a true and actual happening!

'Mum rang up the rescue centre last night,' his dad was telling him, 'and I went and fetched him home first thing this morning. Are you happy now?'

'Happy,' said Patrick.

'A lot, or a little?' his dad asked.

'A lot,' Patrick said.

'And by the way, Patrick,' his mum was saying as they went to the door, 'your dad and me, we've been talking. We thought having a dog might make us get on and really do it.'

'Do what?'

'Get a proper house with a little bit of a garden. We should have done it a long time ago.'

And that was when the giggling started, partly because Best Mate was sitting down on Patrick's chest now, snuffling in his ear, but mostly because he had never been so happy in all his life.

That same morning – it was a Saturday – they

went out and bought a basket for Best Mate, a basket big enough for him to grow into, a bright red lead, a dog bowl and some dog food, and a little collar too with a brass disc hanging from it, engraved with his name and their phone number, just in case Best Mate ever got himself lost. In the afternoon they all walked up the hill through the iron gate and into the park, with Best Mate all tippy-toed and pulling on his lead. Once by the bench at the top of the hill Patrick and Best Mate ran off on their own, down to the pond where they scared the ducks silly, and then back up through the trees to the bench where his mum and dad were waiting. It was better than footie, bike riding, skate-boarding, kite-flying, better than all of them put together. And afterwards they lay down on the crisp autumn leaves, exhausted, and Best Mate gazed up into Patrick's eyes just as he had in the dream, so that Patrick had to squeeze his eyes tight shut and then open them again just to be quite sure that the whole day had really happened.

DAVID COPPERFIELD

by Charles Dickens

I had measles very badly when I was six years old, and had to spend weeks in bed. I wasn't allowed to read in case it strained my eyes, so I was incredibly bored. I played fretful games with my paper dolls and listened to the radio – we didn't have a television then. When my dad came home from work he could sometimes be persuaded to read to me. He valiantly worked his way through all three Faraway Tree *books, and then in desperation went to the set of Dickens novels that stayed unread in the bookcase. He started reading* David Copperfield *aloud.*

I was too young to understand all of it, but I loved the first few chapters, especially the passage where young David plays with little Em'ly in the boathouse at Yarmouth. I laughed at the part where the grown-up David starts courting Dora. She strikes me as a

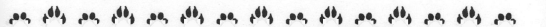

highly irritating heroine now, so coy and girly and helpless – but I still adore her jealous little dog Jip.

The following is the passage where David meets Jip for the first time.

JᴨS

❧ DAVID COPPERFIELD ❧

It was a fine morning, and early, and I thought I would go and take a stroll down one of those wire-arched walks, and indulge my passion by dwelling on her image. On my way through the hall, I encountered her little dog, who was called Jip – short for Gypsy. I approached him tenderly, for I loved even him; but he showed his whole set of teeth, got under a chair expressly to snarl, and wouldn't hear of the least familiarity.

The garden was cool and solitary. I walked about, wondering what my feelings of happiness would be, if I could ever become engaged to this dear wonder. As to marriage, and fortune, and all that, I believe I was almost as innocently undesigning then, as when I loved little Em'ly. To be allowed to call her 'Dora', to write to her, to dote upon and worship her, to have reason to think that when she was with other people she was yet mindful of me, seemed to me the summit of human ambition – I am sure it was the summit of mine. There is no doubt whatever that I was a lackadaisical young spooney; but there was a purity of heart in all this still, that prevents my having quite a contemptuous recollection of it, let me laugh as I may.

I had not been walking long, when I turned a corner and met her. I tingle again from head to foot as my recollection turns that corner, and my pen shakes in my hand.

'You – are – out early, Miss Spenlow,' said I.

'It's so stupid at home,' she replied, 'and Miss Murdstone is so absurd! She talks such nonsense about its being necessary for the day to be aired, before I come out. Aired!' (She laughed, here, in the most melodious manner.) 'On a Sunday morning, when I don't practise, I must do something. So I told Papa last night I *must* come out. Besides, it's the brightest time of the whole day. Don't you think so?'

I hazarded a bold flight, and said (not without stammering) that it was very bright to me then, though it had been very dark to me a minute before.

'Do you mean a compliment?' said Dora, 'or that the weather has really changed?'

I stammered worse than before, in replying that I meant no compliment, but the plain truth; though I was not aware of any change having taken place in the weather. It was in the state of my own feelings, I added bashfully, to clench the explanation.

I never saw such curls – how could I, for there never were such curls! – as those she shook out to hide her blushes. As to the straw hat and blue ribbons which was at the top of the curls, if I could only have hung it up in my room in Buckingham Street, what a priceless possession it would have been!

'You have just come home from Paris,' said I.

'Yes,' said she. 'Have you ever been there?'

'No.'

'Oh! I hope you'll go soon. You would like it so much!'

Traces of deep-seated anguish appeared in my countenance. That she should hope I would go, that she should think it possible I *could* go, was insupportable. I depreciated Paris; I depreciated France. I said I wouldn't leave England, under existing circumstances, for any earthly consideration. Nothing should induce me. In short, she was shaking the curls again, when the little dog came running along the walk to our relief.

He was mortally jealous of me, and persisted in barking at me. She took him up in her arms – oh my goodness! – and caressed him, but he insisted upon barking still. He wouldn't let me touch him, when I tried; and then she beat him. It increased my sufferings greatly to see the pats she gave him for punishment on the bridge of his blunt nose, while he winked his eyes, and licked her hand, and still growled within himself like a little double-bass. At length he was quiet – well he might be with her dimpled chin upon his head! – and we walked away to look at a greenhouse.

'You are not very intimate with Miss Murdstone, are you?' said Dora. 'My pet!'

(The two last words were to the dog. Oh, if they had only been to me!)

'No,' I replied. 'Not at all so.'

'She is a tiresome creature,' said Dora, pouting. 'I can't think what Papa can have been about, when he chose such a vexatious thing to be my companion. Who wants a protector! I am sure *I* don't want a protector. Jip can protect me a great deal better than Miss Murdstone, – can't you, Jip dear?'

He only winked lazily, when she kissed his ball of a head.

'Papa calls her my confidential friend, but I am sure she is no such thing – is she, Jip? We are not going to confide in any such cross people, Jip and I. We mean to bestow our confidence where we like, and to find out our own friends, instead of having them found out for us – don't we, Jip?'

Jip made a comfortable noise, in answer, a little like a tea-kettle when it sings. As for me, every word was a new heap of fetters, rivetted above the last.

'It is very hard, because we have not a kind Mama, that we are to have, instead, a sulky, gloomy old thing like Miss Murdstone, always following us about – isn't it, Jip? Never mind, Jip. We won't be confidential, and we'll make ourselves as happy as we can in spite of her, and we'll tease her, and not please her, – won't we, Jip?'

If it had lasted any longer, I think I must have gone down on my knees on the gravel, with the probability before me of grazing them, and of being presently ejected from the premises besides. But, by good fortune the greenhouse was not far off, and these words brought us to it.

It contained quite a show of beautiful geraniums.

We loitered along in front of them, and Dora often stopped to admire this one or that one, and I stopped to admire the same one, and Dora, laughing, held the dog up childishly, to smell the flowers; and if we were not all three in Fairyland, certainly *I* was. The scent of a geranium leaf, at this day, strikes me with a half comical, half serious wonder as to what change has come over me in a moment; and then I see a straw hat and blue ribbons, and a quantity of curls, and a little black dog being held up, in two slender arms, against a bank of blossoms and bright leaves.

SHADOW, THE SHEEP-DOG

by Enid Blyton

I read at least a hundred Enid Blyton titles between the ages of six and eight. They were such easy-to-read, comforting books. I could take an armful out of the library, race through them all in a week or so, and then rush back for more. I read about strange folk who lived in magic trees, girls in boarding schools, gangs of children having extraordinary adventures, and colourful circus stories.

One of my favourite Blyton books was Shadow, the Sheep-Dog. *I was given it as a birthday present when I was seven and read it over and over again. It's an ordinary enough story about a boy called Johnny who lives on a farm and has his own collie sheep-dog, but it seemed wonderfully exciting to me. I'd have given*

*anything to live in the country in those days – and I
particularly wanted my own dog.*

*Shadow is called a Wonder Dog in the story, and
he's almost impossibly clever, brave and loyal. That's
the whole charm of the story. You don't ever have to
worry reading an Enid Blyton book. You know that
things will always work out well eventually in her reas-
suring fictional world. Shadow will unerringly rescue
Johnny, and find the lost lamb, and chase off the rats
and the fox and the eagle. When a rich American wants
to buy Shadow to turn him into a film star like Lassie,
and little Johnny is prepared to let him go to save
his father's farm, it gets a little tense, especially when
there's an unfortunate accident and poor Shadow is
nearly blinded. However, this means he isn't shipped
off to Hollywood after all and, surprise surprise, he
makes a complete recovery.*

*If you fancy reading the whole story when you've
read this extract, I'm sure you'll be able to find an old
copy in a second-hand bookshop.*

Jw

🐾 SHADOW, THE 🐾 SHEEP-DOG

Johnny Gets into Trouble

One Saturday, when Johnny had a holiday from school, he wanted to go nutting on High-Over Hill with the other boys.

'But you can't possibly walk there!' said his mother.

'I could borrow Will's bike,' said Johnny. 'I can ride a bike. Let me go, Mother. It will be such fun.'

His father looked up from the newspaper he was reading.

'High-Over Hill is dangerous,' he said. 'I remember your uncle falling down the steep side of it when he went nutting as a boy – and he broke his leg. If you go, you must keep on the west side – that's not dangerous.'

'All right, Dad,' said Johnny, beaming. 'Can I borrow Will's bike, then?'

'Yes, if you take care of it, and clean it when you come back,' said his father. 'You must remember that if you borrow things you must always return them clean and in good condition.'

'Can I take Shadow with me?' asked Johnny.

'No,' said his father. 'Shadow has work to do with the sheep this morning – and anyway I don't want him running along the roads all the way to High-Over Hill. It's too far.'

'But Shadow wouldn't mind,' said Johnny, looking sad all of a sudden, for he hated spending a day without Shadow. 'Shadow would like it. Oh, please give him a holiday too, Dad!'

'Shadow is already at work,' said the farmer, nodding towards the window.

Johnny looked out. Sure enough, he could see Shadow on the far hill, running with the other dogs, separating the sheep out into little flocks for the shepherd. Some were to go to market that day, and the dogs were helping to bunch the sheep.

Johnny said no more. He had been taught not to argue with his parents. He thought he would get Will's bike, and then he would go up to the hill where Shadow was at work, and explain to him that he couldn't take him with him that day.

Will was one of the farm-hands. He was quite willing to lend Johnny his bike, for the boy was careful. Johnny looked to see if the brakes were all right, thanked Will, and then jumped on the bike. Off he went, cycling up the path that led to the hill where the sheep were grazing.

Shadow came bounding to meet him. He had already seen Johnny that morning, for he had slept on the boy's bed the night before. But when he had heard the shepherd whistling to the other dogs he had licked Johnny's sleepy face, and had run out of the door. He was Johnny's dog – but he had to work for his living just as the other dogs did!

'Shadow, I'm going off for the day,' said Johnny. 'I'm going nutting.'

Shadow looked at Johnny and the bike. He understood quite well what the boy meant. He wagged his plumy tail joyfully. How he loved going off for the day with Johnny!

'Don't look so pleased about it,' said Johnny. 'I've

got to go without you. You can't come today, Shadow. I've just come up here to say goodbye to you. I'll be back by tea-time.'

Shadow's tail drooped down. All the wag went out of it. What – Johnny was going off without him! He looked up at the boy with mournful brown eyes.

'Don't look at me like that, Shadow,' said Johnny, 'else I shan't be able to go. You see, Dad says you have work to do today. So I can't have you with me. But cheer up – I'll be back by tea-time. I promise!'

Shadow wagged his tail just a tiny bit. He was very sad – but he didn't want to stop Johnny from having a happy day. The shepherd whistled to the dogs, and Shadow had to bound off. He licked Johnny's hand, barked to tell him to be sure and have a good day, and then leapt off to join Tinker and Rafe.

Johnny rode over the hill on his bicycle. He soon joined the other boys, and they shouted to one another.

'Gorgeous day!' yelled Ronnie.

'What have you got for your lunch?' shouted Harry. 'I've got ham sandwiches, and the biggest bit of chocolate cake you ever saw.'

'Have you all brought baskets for the nuts?' said Johnny. 'I've got one. I hope I get it full. My dad loves hazel nuts. He eats them with salt.'

The boys rode off together happily. It was a long way to High-Over Hill, but it was quite the best place for nutting. There were hundreds of fine nut-trees there.

One of the boys got a puncture in his back tyre. All of them jumped off to help. Johnny found a puncture-mending outfit in the saddle-bag at the back of his bike, and very soon the puncture was mended.

Then off they all went again, chattering and shouting. When they came to the place where they meant to go nutting, they jumped off their bicycles, laid them on the grass, and ran to the trees.

'Golly! I never in my life saw so many nuts before!' cried Harry eagerly. 'Just look at them! My word, they are beauties! Let's pick some to have with our lunch, shall we? Then we can set to work properly after that, and fill our baskets.'

The boys plucked the clusters of nuts. What fine ones they were! Then they sat down and undid their packets of sandwiches and cake. How they enjoyed them! Most of them had brought something to drink as well. Then they ate their nuts. Harry had actually brought a pair of nut-crackers, which everyone voted a very clever thing to do. But some of the boys, who had very strong teeth, preferred to crack the nuts in their mouths.

'All very well for *you*,' said Harry, cracking his nuts with crackers. 'But my teeth aren't very good – and I'm not going to risk breaking them, I can tell you.'

After lunch the boys took up their baskets and went nutting. Some of them had sticks with crooked handles so that they might pull down the higher branches.

Harry went over the top of the hill. He gave a shout. 'I say! The trees on this side are marvellous! What about picking some of the nuts from here?'

But the other boys were too busy picking from the other trees, so Harry went to join them. Johnny was doing a funny thing. He hadn't a stick to pull down the high branches – so he fetched his bicycle, and propped it up against a nut tree, and now he was standing on the saddle so that he could reach the fine clusters above his head.

When he had picked all he could see, he left his bicycle under the tree and went to the top of the hill. He just wanted to see over, down the other side. And, of course, when he got there, he spied the trees that Harry had seen, so full of nuts that the branches hung almost to the ground. The hillside was very steep, and nobody had dared to risk getting the nuts from the trees there. So there were hundreds and hundreds.

Johnny forgot that he had been told not to pick

nuts on the steep side of the hill. His eyes shone with delight as he thought of how he could fill his basket to the brim with enormous nuts. He began to climb down the steep side of the hill towards the clump of hazels.

The earth on the hillside was loose. Stones rolled down as Johnny scrambled along. Then he slipped and clutched at a tuft of grass. But the grass was not strong enough to hold him, and came out by the roots. Johnny fell headlong down the hill, bumping into rocks and stones as he went, trying to clutch at trees and bushes, but just missing them.

He fell with a crash to the bottom, hit his head on a stone, and then lay still, with his eyes closed. He had not shouted, because he had been too frightened, so the other boys did not know he had fallen.

Harry and the others picked nuts steadily. The boys were spread out well on the other side of the hill, and nobody missed Johnny. They all thought he was somewhere with them. It was only when it was time to go home that they missed him.

'It's four o'clock,' said Harry. 'We'd better be starting back. Let's get our bikes. Anyway, we can't possibly get any more nuts into our baskets or our pockets either!'

Every boy had his basket full, and his pockets too.

They were very pleased with their afternoon's work. They picked up their bicycles and were about to jump on them, when Harry looked all round in surprise.

'Where's Johnny?' he said.

Johnny was certainly not with them. Harry shouted loudly, 'Johnny! Johnny! We're going now! Hurry up!'

There was no answer. Then Ronnie spoke in surprise. 'He must have gone home, because his bike isn't here! There are only our bikes – not Johnny's. He must have slipped off before us.'

'So he must,' said Harry. 'Well, what a funny thing to do! He might have waited! Come on. We must hurry now.'

Off went the boys, whistling and chattering, never knowing that Johnny's bike was under a hazel tree where he had left it – and that Johnny himself was lying with his eyes still closed at the bottom of High-Over Hill. Nobody worried about him at all.

Nobody? Yes – there was somebody worrying dreadfully! And that was Shadow. Shadow loved Johnny so much that he knew when things were going wrong with him. And poor Shadow was sitting anxiously on the hillside at the farm, watching and watching for a boy who didn't come. What was to be done about it?

Good Dog, Shadow

Shadow sat and waited, his eyes turned towards the lane down which Johnny should come. Rafe ran up to him.

'What's the matter? Why is your tail down?'

'I'm unhappy,' said Shadow. 'I feel that something is wrong with Johnny. I know there is!'

Rafe knew what Shadow meant. He looked towards the lane too. 'Maybe Johnny will come along soon,' he said. 'Perhaps his bicycle has broken.'

'I wish Johnny wouldn't go out without me,' said Shadow. 'I can look after him when I am with him.'

Rafe sat down to keep Shadow company. Dandy came up too, and the three dogs sat together in silence.

Then, at five o'clock, they saw Johnny's mother come out of the farmhouse to look up the lane to see if Johnny was anywhere about.

'Johnny! Johnny!' she called. 'Are you back yet?'

Will came by, carrying a pitchfork over his shoulder. 'I don't think Master Johnny's home yet, Mam,' he said. 'He said he'd bring me my bicycle as soon as he got in, because I wanted it myself this evening – and he hasn't come.'

'Oh dear! I wonder what has happened,' said

Johnny's mother anxiously. 'It's past tea-time now – and Johnny promised to be home.'

Shadow darted down the hill and ran up to Johnny's mother. He looked up at her with dark, worried eyes.

'So you are anxious too,' said the farmer's wife. 'What has happened to Johnny, Shadow? Can't you find him for me?'

Shadow barked and then whined. If only he *could* find Johnny!

He ran to Rafe. 'Where is High-Over Hill, where Johnny has gone?' he asked. 'Have I ever been there?'

'No,' said Rafe. 'But do you remember where we once took some sheep to Farmer Langdon? Well, High-Over Hill is just past there – you can see it when you pass the farm – a great big hill sticking up into the sky.'

'I shall find it,' said Shadow. 'But what a long way it is! Goodbye, Rafe. I don't know when I shall be back.'

Shadow set off. He did not go the way that Johnny had gone, up the lane and along the road. No – Shadow knew the short-cuts among the hills. He ran along swiftly, smelling the well-known scents of rabbit, fox, weasel, hare, and stoat as he went. How he wished he could suddenly smell Johnny too!

It was a long way to Langdon's farm, even by the short-cuts. But Shadow did not once think of being tired, although he had done a hard day's work. All his mind was full of Johnny. He must find Johnny. He must, he must. He knew in his faithful heart that Johnny was in trouble. Something had happened to Johnny. He was sure of it.

He came at last to Langdon's farm. The sun was setting. It would soon be dark. Shadow trotted quickly down the lane past the farm. He did not dare take the short-cut through the farmyard itself, because the farm-dogs would set on him. No dog allows another on his own farm without the farmer's permission.

Some way ahead, outlined against the evening sky, was High-Over Hill. Shadow ran even more swiftly. Something told him that Johnny was there.

The dog ran up the slope of the hill – and suddenly his heart beat quickly. He could smell Johnny's scent! Johnny had been there, no doubt about that.

The dog nosed about the trees – and suddenly he found Johnny's bicycle, leaning against one of the hazels. He sniffed at it. Then he nosed about to find the boy's footprints. He found plenty of them, leading here and there. Shadow followed them with his nose – and at last he found footprints leading to the top of the hill.

Shadow followed them. He came to where Johnny had begun to climb down the hill – he came to where Johnny had slipped and fallen – and then, on the breeze, there came such a strong smell of Johnny that Shadow lifted his head and barked loudly:

'Johnny! I'm here!'

And a feeble voice answered from the bottom of the hill: 'Shadow! Oh, Shadow!'

Shadow leapt down that hill in a trice! He cared nothing for stones and rocks. Only one thing filled his heart and mind – he had found his beloved little master again. Johnny! Johnny!

In two seconds the big sheep-dog was beside the boy, licking his hands, his face, his legs, anywhere that he could find to lick. He whined as he licked Johnny, and the boy put both his arms round the big dog's neck.

'Oh, Shadow! I'm hurt and I've been so frightened and lonely here all by myself. Oh, Shadow, I did want you so! How did you find me? Shadow, don't leave me.'

Shadow sat down beside Johnny. He was happy again now that he had found his master. But he was worried too. How could he get help for Johnny without leaving him? He couldn't get anyone if he didn't leave Johnny to fetch help. Yet the boy was so frightened and lonely. Shadow could not bear to leave him. His head was bleeding too. Shadow licked the bad place gently to make it clean. The boy curled up close to the dog for warmth, for he was very cold.

Shadow lay as close as he could. He could feel Johnny getting warmer and warmer. That was good. It was getting dark now. Shadow heard Johnny's breathing and knew that he was asleep. Perhaps he could leave the boy for a short while and go to Langdon's farm for help?

He slipped gradually away. Johnny was tired and still slept on. Shadow ran round the hill and went to the farm. The farm-dogs set up a tremendous barking. The farmer came into the yard to see what the noise was about. Shadow ran to him and tugged at his coat.

The farmer flashed his lantern down and saw the big sheep-dog. 'Why, if it isn't Johnny's Shadow!' he cried in amazement. 'What do you want here, Shadow?'

Shadow barked and ran to the farm-gate. The farmer knew at once that the dog wanted him to follow. He went back to the farmhouse and fetched a coat. Then he set out behind Shadow.

'Don't go so fast!' he called. 'I can't see my way as well as you can!'

But Shadow was impatient to get back to Johnny.

Suppose the boy had awakened and had missed him? How upset he would be!

Soon he and the farmer were beside the hurt boy. Johnny awoke and shivered, puzzled to see the lantern shining down on him. Then he groaned because his head ached so badly.

'Well, old son, so you've had a bit of a fall, have you?' said Farmer Langdon. 'I'll carry you back to my farm. Your dog fetched me. Ah, he's a marvel, that dog of yours!'

'He found me,' said Johnny. 'Oh, I was glad when I heard him bark. It was the nicest sound in the world!'

The farmer carried the boy gently back to the farm. Mrs Langdon bathed his head and his ankle, which had been badly sprained. Then she telephoned to his mother to tell her what had happened.

'We'll keep him here tonight,' she said. 'He is quite all right now, except for a bad head and a swollen ankle. We've got Shadow here too.'

'*Shadow!*' said Johnny's mother in astonishment. 'How did *he* get there? He didn't go with Johnny today.'

'Well, he found him at the bottom of High-Over Hill,' said Mrs Langdon. 'He came to fetch my husband, and that's how we got Johnny! He's a wonderful dog.'

'Dear old Shadow!' said Johnny's mother, her eyes full of tears. 'I don't know what we would do without him.'

Johnny stayed at the farm that night, and slept in the spare room there, with Shadow as usual stretched over his feet. It was the first time that Shadow had slept in another house, but he didn't mind where he slept so long as he was with Johnny.

The boy was taken home the next day, and his mother hugged him. His father welcomed him too, and the boy told him how the accident happened.

'I disobeyed you, Dad,' he said. 'But I didn't mean to. I quite forgot what you had said about not going over the steep side of the hill. But I've been well punished for it. And if it hadn't been for Shadow, I don't know what would have happened to me!'

'Good dog, Shadow!' said Johnny's father, and he patted the big dog. 'Good dog! I'll let you off your work for two or three days so that you can be with Johnny whilst he is getting better. Look after him, won't you?'

Of course Shadow would! It was the thing he loved best in the world.

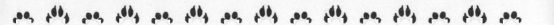

THE KNIFE OF NEVER LETTING GO

by Patrick Ness

The Knife of Never Letting Go *is the first book in an amazingly inventive and exciting trilogy set in a terrifying future. Have you ever longed to be able to read someone's thoughts to find out what they really think of you? In Patrick Ness's New World all the men can read each other's thoughts – but you realize this would be appalling and deafening and dangerous in real life. The hero Todd frequently has to endeavour to block his Noise, with little success. He's in constant danger – but there are some wonderful funny or charming moments in the book too. Animals can talk, but not in long elaborate sentences. They retain all their animal qualities: the crickets cheep Sex sex sex, the sheep placidly baa Sheep sheep sheep, and*

the huge herd of extraordinary enormous cattle sing
Here I am, here I am.

Todd's dog Manchee frequently has very basic
needs on his canine mind. Todd doesn't always appreciate him at first, finding him irritating, but as the
book progresses he realizes that Manchee is a wonderful, valiant friend. The Knife of Never Letting
Go is easy to read, but I think you have to be quite
grown up to deal with its subject matter. Soft-hearted
animal lovers might find it unbearable!

Jw

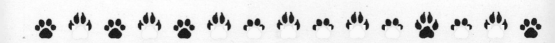

❧ THE KNIFE OF NEVER ❧ LETTING GO

'We gotta stop,' I say, dropping the rucksack at the base of a tree. 'We gotta rest.'

The girl sets her own bag down by another tree without needing any more convincing and we both just sort of collapse down, leaning on our bags like pillows.

'Five minutes,' I say. Manchee curls up by my legs and closes his eyes almost immediately. 'Only five minutes,' I call over to the girl, who's pulled a little blanket outta her bag to cover herself with. 'Don't get too comfortable.'

We gotta keep going, no question of that. I'll only close my eyes for a minute or two, just to get a little rest, and then we'll keep on going faster than before.

Just a little rest, that's all.

I open my eyes and the sun is up. Only a little but ruddy well up.

Crap. We've lost at least an hour, maybe two.

And then I realize it's a sound that's woken me.

It's Noise.

I panic, thinking of men finding us and I scramble to my feet—

Only to see that it ain't a man.

It's a cassor, towering over me and Manchee and the girl.

Food? says its Noise.

I *knew* they hadn't left the swamp.

I hear a little gasp from over where the girl's sleeping. Not sleeping no more. The cassor turns to look at her. And then Manchee's up and barking, 'Get! Get! Get!' and the cassor's neck swings back our way.

Imagine the biggest bird you ever saw, imagine it got so big that it couldn't even fly no more, we're talking two and a half or even three metres tall, a super long bendy neck stretching up way over yer head. It's still got feathers but they look more

366

like fur and the wings ain't good for much except stunning things they're about to eat. But it's the feet you gotta watch out for. Long legs, up to my chest, with claws at the end that can kill you with one kick if yer not careful.

'Don't worry,' I call over to the girl. 'They're friendly.'

Cuz they are. Or they're sposed to be. They're sposed to eat rodents and only kick if you attack 'em, but if you *don't* attack 'em, Ben says they're friendly and dopey and'll let you feed 'em. And they're also good to eat, a combo which made the new settlers of Prentisstown so eager to hunt 'em for food that by the time I was born there wasn't a cassor to be seen within miles. Yet another thing I only ever saw in a vid or Noise.

The world keeps getting bigger.

'Get! Get!' Manchee barks, running in a circle round the cassor.

'Don't bite it!' I shout at him.

The cassor's neck is swinging about like a vine, following Manchee around like a cat after a bug. **Food?** its Noise keeps asking.

'Not food,' I say, and the big neck swings my way. **Food?**

'Not food,' I say again. 'Just a dog.'

Dog? it thinks and starts following Manchee around again, trying to nip him with his beak. The beak ain't a scary thing at all, like being nipped by a goose, but Manchee's having none of it, leaping outta the way and barking, barking, barking.

I laugh at him. It's funny.

And then I hear a little laugh that ain't my own.

I look over. The girl is standing by her tree, watching the giant bird chase around my stupid dog, and she's laughing.

She's *smiling*.

She sees me looking and she stops.

Food? I hear and I turn to see the cassor starting to poke its beak into my rucksack.

'Hey!' I shout and start shooing it away.

Food?

'Here.' I fish out a small block of cheese wrapped in a cloth that Ben packed.

The cassor sniffs it, bites it, and gobbles it down, its neck rippling in long waves as it swallows. It snaps its beak a few times like a man might smack his lips after he ate something. But then its neck starts rippling the other way and with a loud hack, up comes the block of cheese flying right back at me, covered in spit but not hardly even crushed, smacking me on the cheek and leaving a trail of slime across my face.

Food? says the cassor and starts slowly walking off into the swamp, as if we're no longer even as interesting as a leaf.

'Get! Get!' Manchee barks after it, but not following. I wipe the slime from my face with my sleeve and I can see the girl smiling at me while I do it.

'Think that's funny, do ya?' I say and she keeps pretending like she's not smiling but she *is*. She turns away and picks up her bag.

'Yeah,' I say, taking charge of things again. 'We slept way too long. We gotta go.'

BECAUSE OF WINN-DIXIE

by Kate DiCamillo

This is a lovely book, very moving and delicately moral. Opal and her dog Winn-Dixie make friends with all sorts of extraordinary and interesting characters, but my favourite is Miss Franny Block, who's in charge of the Herman W. Block Memorial Library. When she was a little girl her father, who was very rich, said she could have anything she wanted for her birthday. Anything at all.

What would you ask for? Miss Franny loves to read so she asks for a small library. She says, 'I wanted a little house full of nothing but books and I wanted to share them, too. And I got my wish. My father built me this house, the very one we are sitting in now. And at a very young age I became a librarian.'

I think that's what I'd have wished for too. Miss Franny is 'a very small, very old woman with short grey hair' – and so am I now. And I have my own library of around fifteen thousand books, lovingly collected over many years.

JW

🐾 BECAUSE OF 🐾 WINN-DIXIE

My name is India Opal Buloni, and last summer my daddy, the preacher, sent me to the store for a box of macaroni-and-cheese, some white rice and two tomatoes, and I came back with a dog.

This is what happened: I walked into the produce section of the Winn-Dixie grocery store to pick out my two tomatoes and I almost bumped right into the store manager. He was standing there all red-faced, screaming and waving his arms around.

'Who let a dog in here?' he kept on shouting. 'Who let a dirty dog in here?'

At first, I didn't see a dog. There were just a lot of vegetables rolling around on the floor, tomatoes and onions and green peppers. And there was what seemed like a whole army of Winn-Dixie employees running around waving their arms just the same way the store manager was waving his.

And then the dog came running around the corner. He was a big dog. And ugly. And he looked like he was having a real good time. His tongue was hanging out and he was wagging his tail. He skidded to a stop and smiled right at me. I had never before in my life seen a dog smile, but that is what he did. He pulled back his lips and showed me all his teeth. Then he wagged his tail so hard that he knocked some oranges off a display and they went rolling everywhere, mixing in with the tomatoes and onions and green peppers.

The manager screamed, 'Somebody grab that dog!'

The dog went running over to the manager, wagging his tail and smiling. He stood up on his hind legs. You could tell that all he wanted to do was get face to face with the manager and thank him for the good time he was having in the produce department, but somehow he ended up knocking the manager over. And the manager must have been having a bad day because, lying there on the floor, right in front of everybody, he started to cry. The dog leaned over him, real concerned, and licked his face.

'Please,' said the manager, 'somebody call the pound.'

'Wait a minute!' I hollered. 'That's my dog. Don't call the pound.'

All the Winn-Dixie employees turned around and looked at me, and I knew I had done something big. And maybe stupid, too. But I couldn't help it. I couldn't let that dog go to the pound.

'Here, boy,' I said.

The dog stopped licking the manager's face and put his ears up in the air and looked at me, like he was trying to remember where he knew me from.

'Here, boy,' I said again. And then I figured that the dog was probably just like everybody else in the world, that he would want to get called by a name, only I didn't know what his name was, so I just said the first thing that came into my head. I said, 'Here, Winn-Dixie.'

And that dog came trotting over to me just like he had been doing it his whole life.

The manager sat up and gave me a hard stare, like maybe I was making fun of him.

'It's his name,' I said. 'Honest.'

The manager said, 'Don't you know not to bring a dog into a grocery store?'

'Yes, sir,' I told him. 'He got in by mistake. I'm sorry. It won't happen again.'

'Come on, Winn-Dixie,' I said to the dog.

I started walking and he followed along behind me as I went out of the produce department and down the cereal aisle and past all the cashiers and out the door.

Once we were safe outside, I checked him over real careful and he didn't look that good. He was big, but skinny; you could see his ribs. And there were bald patches all over him, places where he didn't have any fur at all. Mostly, he looked like a big piece of old brown carpet that had been left out in the rain.

'You're a mess,' I told him. 'I bet you don't belong to anybody.'

He smiled at me. He did that thing again, where he pulled back his lips and showed me his teeth. He smiled so big that it made him sneeze. It was like he was saying, 'I know I'm a mess. Isn't it funny?'

It's hard not to immediately fall in love with a dog who has a good sense of humour.

'Come on,' I told him. 'Let's see what the preacher has to say about you.'

And the two of us, me and Winn-Dixie, started walking home.

THE WEREPUPPY

by Jacqueline Wilson

I wrote The Werepuppy *over twenty years ago – one of my few books where the main character is a boy. Micky isn't a very* boyish *boy. He's very quiet and gentle, and loves drawing and colouring and making up his own Magic Land. He's very wary of three things: his annoying sisters, horror films about werewolves, and dogs. He's become so scared of dogs that his mum decides to get him a puppy. Micky is appalled at the idea – but he's in for a surprise!*

I decided to have fun when I described the dogs at the dog shelter, basing them on real animals. I mentioned a Scottie called Jeannie – she belonged to a teacher friend of mine called Holly. I also wrote very fondly about a cream Labrador called Tumble. She belonged to my dear friend Peter. (She'd had a sister called Rough, though she'd always lived with someone else.)

Peter and Tumble were inseparable. Tumble lolloped into the back of Peter's car and went with him to work. She trotted along to the pub with Peter every evening and was allowed her own packet of crisps for supper. She could bite them open and wolf the contents down in less than a minute. It's probably not the most sensible thing to feed your dog, but Tumble lived until she was an ancient old lady, serene and good natured till the end.

Peter himself died three years ago, and I like to think that in some other world they are both still ambling down to the pub for whatever the afterlife sees fit to serve – a pint of nectar and a packet of ambrosia-flavoured crisps?

J~S

🐾 THE WEREPUPPY 🐾

'Please, Mum,' Micky begged. 'I can't go in there!'

Mum wouldn't listen. She made Micky get out of the car.

She knocked on the front door of the dogs' home. The howling increased, and then there was a lot of barking too. Micky clung to Mum's arm, and even Marigold took a step backwards. The door opened and a young freckled woman in jeans stood there smiling, surrounded by two barking Labradors, the colour of clotted cream, and a small black Scottie who kept diving through the Labradors' legs.

'Quiet, you silly dogs,' the woman shouted. She saw Micky shrinking away and said quickly, 'It's OK, they're all very friendly. They won't bite. There's no need to be frightened of them.'

'*I'm* not frightened,' said Marigold, squatting down to pet the Scottie, while the two Labradors sniffed and nuzzled. 'Aren't they lovely? What are their names? Shall we have the little Scottie dog, Mum? Although I like the big creamy dogs too. Oh look, this one's *smiling* at me.'

'That's Tumble. And that's her brother Rough.'

'Oh great. We're a sister and brother and we can *have* a sister dog and brother dog.'

'No, I'm afraid Rough and Tumble are my dogs. And wee Jeannie here. But there are plenty of other lovely dogs to choose from out the back. I've got lots of strays at the moment. Come through to the kennels.'

'I'll wait outside,' Micky hissed, trying to dodge Rough and Tumble's big wet licks.

'Don't be silly, Micky,' said Mum. 'This is going to be your dog. You've got to choose.'

'I'll choose for him,' said Marigold, still playing with Jeannie. She rolled over and let Marigold tickle her tummy. 'There, look! She loves being tickled, doesn't she? It's my magic trick of taming all dogs. Maybe I'll be a dog trainer in a circus as well as a bare-back rider.'

'I think it's a trick that only works with little friendly dogs like Jeannie,' said Miss Webb. 'You shouldn't even touch some of the big dogs I've got out the back, just in case.'

'I'm not scared of any dogs, even really big ones,' Marigold boasted. 'Not like my brother. He's older than me too, and yet he's *ever* so scared.'

'No I'm not,' Micky said hoarsely, but at that moment Jeannie nudged against his leg and he gave a little yelp of terror.

'See that!' said Marigold triumphantly. 'He's even scared of a little Scottie. He's hopeless, isn't he? I don't know why Mum wants to get him a dog, it's just daft, isn't it? She ought to get *me* a dog, seeing as I'm the one that likes them. And dogs don't need a special stable, do they? Just a little kennel.'

'Or even an old cardboard box,' said Miss Webb. 'I've got special big kennels at the back of my house because I always have so many stray dogs on my hands.' She turned back to Micky. 'But it's OK, they're all in separate pens and they can't get out.'

'He'll still be scared,' said Marigold. 'He's even scared of me.' She suddenly darted at Micky, going woof-woof-woof and poor Micky was so strung up and startled by this time that he jumped and very nearly burst into tears.

'Marigold!' said Mum, but she gave Micky a shake too, obviously embarrassed.

Marigold just laughed and Miss Webb was trying hard to keep a straight face. Micky blinked desperately, and tried to swallow the lump in his throat. His face was scarlet, his whole body burning.

'We've got some puppies out the back,' said Miss Webb. 'They're really sweet and cuddly. I'd have a puppy if I were you.'

Micky's throat ached so much he could barely speak.

'I don't really want any dog. Not even a puppy, thank you,' he croaked.

'Just take a look, Micky,' said Mum, giving him a little push.

So Micky had to go with them to the kennels at the back of the house. The howling got louder. It had a strange eerie edge to it. Marigold put her hands over her ears.

'Which one's making that horrid noise?' she complained.

'Yes, sorry. That's a stray we picked up last night. He's been making that row ever since, though we've done our best to comfort him. He's only a puppy, but he's a vicious little thing all the same. I certainly wouldn't recommend him for a family pet, especially as the little boy's so nervous.'

'I bet I could tame him,' Marigold boasted. She approached the pen in the corner, where a big grey puppy stood tensely, head back, howling horribly.

'Nice doggie,' said Marigold, and the puppy quivered and then stopped in mid-howl.

'See that!' said Marigold excitedly. 'There, I've stopped him. He's coming over to see me. Here, boy. You like me, don't you? Do you want to be my doggie, eh? You can't be Micky's dog because he's such a silly little wet wimp.'

Micky couldn't stand the word wimp. It sounded so horrible and feeble and ugly and pimply.

'Don't call Micky silly names,' said Mum.

'Well, it's true. He really *is* a wimp. Even Dad says so,' said Marigold, reaching through the bars to pat the strange grey puppy. 'Dad says I should have been his boy because I've got all the spark, while Micky's just a wimp.'

Micky burned all over. He shut his eyes, his whole skin prickling, itching unbearably. He could still hear the howling but now it seemed to be right inside his own head. He ground his teeth . . . and then suddenly Marigold screamed.

Micky opened his eyes. He stared at his shrieking sister. The grey puppy had a fierce grip of her finger and was biting hard with his little razor teeth.

'Get it off me! Help, help! Oh, Mum, help, it hurts!' Marigold yelled.

A very naughty little grin bared Micky's teeth – almost as if he was biting too. Then he shook his head and Marigold managed to snatch her finger away from the savage little pup.

'*Bad* boy,' said Miss Webb to the excited puppy. 'I'm so sorry he went for you, dear. Mind you, I did try to warn you. You mustn't ever take silly risks with stray dogs. Let's have a look at that finger and see what damage has been done.'

'It's bleeding!' Marigold screamed.

'Come on now, lovey, it's only a little scratch,' said Mum, giving her a cuddle.

'Still, it's better not to take any risks. We'll give it a dab of disinfectant and find you a bandage,' said Miss Webb.

She led the wailing Marigold back into the house. Mum followed, looking a little agitated.

Micky didn't follow. He stayed where he was, out by the dog pens. He took no notice of all the ordinary dogs, obedient in their pens. He didn't even give the cute Labrador puppies snuggled in their basket a second glance. He only had eyes for the strange grey puppy that had bitten Marigold.

It ran towards Micky. Micky didn't back away.

He didn't feel so scared. And the puppy seemed to have perked up too. He didn't howl any more. He made little friendly snuffling sounds.

'You just bit my sister,' Micky whispered.

The puppy coughed several times. It sounded almost as if he was chuckling. Micky started giggling too.

'That was bad,' Micky spluttered, his hand over his mouth so they wouldn't hear back in the house. 'But we don't care, do we?'

The puppy shook his head. He came right up against the bars of his pen, sticking out his soft pointed snout. His amber eyes were wide and trusting now.

'Are you trying to make friends?' Micky asked.

The puppy snuffled.

'Hello, puppy,' Micky said, and he reached through the bars to pat the puppy's head, though Marigold had just demonstrated that this was a very dangerous thing to do.

'But you're not going to bite me, are you?' said Micky.

The puppy twitched his nose and blinked his eyes. Micky very gently touched the coarse grey fur. His hand was trembling. The puppy quivered too, but stayed still. Micky held his breath and started stroking very softly. The puppy pressed up even closer, in spite of the hard bars. His pink tongue came out and he licked Micky's bare knee.

'We're pals, right?' Micky whispered.

The puppy licked several times.

'Hey, I'm not a lollipop,' Micky giggled, wiping at his slobbery knee.

The puppy licked harder, sharing the joke. He managed to get one paw through the bars. He held it out to Micky. Micky shook the hard little pad solemnly.

'How do you do,' said Micky. 'I'm Micky. And that silly girl you bit was my sister Marigold.'

The puppy grinned wolfishly.

'You didn't half go for her, didn't you,' said Micky, and they had another giggle together, the puppy giving little barks of glee.

'Micky! Get away from that dog!' Mum suddenly cried, rushing out of the back of the house. 'How can you be so stupid? Look what he just did to Marigold.'

'He won't bite me,' said Micky calmly.

'Do as your mum says,' said Miss Webb, returning with Marigold. Marigold was still blotched with tears and she held her bandaged finger high in the air to show it off. 'That puppy is much too unpredictable. I don't know what I'm going to do with him.'

'I'll take him as my pet,' said Micky, and the puppy stiffened and then licked him rapturously.

'Don't be silly, Micky,' said Mum, trying to pull him away.

'I'm not being silly, Mum. I want this dog,' said Micky.

'No!' Marigold protested. 'We're not having that horrible mangy nasty thing. It bites. My finger hurts and hurts. I shall maybe have to go to the hospital to get it all stitched up.'

'Marigold, I told you, it's only a scratch,' said Mum. 'Now, Micky, leave that bad puppy alone and come and look at some of the other dogs.'

'No, Mum. I want this one. Please. I must have this puppy.'

'What about these other puppies over here? They're half Labradors and they're very gentle and docile. Look at the little black one with the big eyes. He'd make a much better pet. See, he's much prettier than that puppy there,' said Miss Webb.

'I don't mind him not being pretty. I like the way he looks,' said Micky, and he had both arms through the bars now, holding the puppy tight.

'Micky, will you leave go of him?' said Mum. 'You're really the weirdest little boy. One minute you're scared stiff of all dogs and then the next you make friends with the most vicious little creature. What is it, anyway? Alsatian?'

'It's certainly mostly German shepherd but it's got something else mixed up with it. Something very odd,' said Miss Webb.

'I know,' said Micky, nodding solemnly. 'And I want him so. Oh, Mum, please, please, please.'

'No, he's not to have him, Mum! He'll bite me again,' Marigold protested furiously.

Mum dithered between the two of them, looking helpless. Micky looked up at her, his big brown eyes glinting amber in the sunlight.

'You said it was going to be my pet. I had to choose him. And I've chosen,' said Micky.

Mum sighed. 'All right, then. You can have that one if you really must. Only I still think it's a very silly choice.'

Micky knew it was the only possible choice. He had the most magical pet in the whole world. His very own werewolf. Well, not quite a werewolf yet. A werepuppy.

About Battersea Dogs & Cats Home...

Battersea Dogs & Cats Home is one of the oldest and most famous animal rescue centres in the world. Founded by a Victorian lady, Mrs Mary Tealby, in 1860, Battersea's dream is of every dog and cat enjoying a loving, permanent and safe home. Until that happens, Battersea aims never to turn away an animal in need.

Battersea rescues, rehabilitates and rehomes dogs and cats who are abandoned, neglected or unwanted, and looks after them while new homes are found. In 2012, 5,880 dogs and 2,760 cats were cared for at the Home's three centres in London, Old Windsor in Berkshire and Brands Hatch in Kent. Over 1,000 volunteers and 300 staff make sure every animal who comes to Battersea's gate gets the love, care and medical treatment they need.

Discover more about Battersea's history
and work at **battersea.org.uk**

Help us care for lost and frightened animals by donating to Battersea at **battersea.org.uk/donate**

Find out how to rehome a dog or cat at
battersea.org.uk/rehoming